Miracle in Music City

Other books by Natalie Grant

Glimmer Girls series

London Art Chase (Book One)
A Dolphin Wish (Book Two)

faithgirlz

Miracle in Music City

by Natalie Grant
with Naomi Kinsman

ZONDERkidz™

ZONDERKIDZ

Miracle in Music City
Copyright © 2016 by Natalie Grant
Illustrations © 2016 by Cathi Mingus

This title is also available as a Zondervan ebook. Visit www.zondervan.com/ebooks

This title is also available in a Zondervan audio edition. Visit www.zondervan.fm

Requests for information should be addressed to:
Zonderkidz, 3900 Sparks Drive, Grand Rapids, Michigan 49546

ISBN 978-0-310-75250-9

Art direction: Cindy Davis
Cover design and interior illustrations: Cathi Mingus
Content contributor: Naomi Kinsman
Interior design: Denise Froehlich

Printed in the United States of America

18 19 20 21 22 /LSC/ 20 19 18 17 16 15 14 13 12 11 10 9 8 7 6 5

To my Glimmer Girls—Gracie, Bella, and Sadie.
You're my greatest adventure. I love you.

Thank you to Naomi Kinsman for bringing your genius creativity and beautiful patience to this process. None of this would be a reality without you.

ONE

Race you to the tree!" Annabeth shouted the minute they were out the door for recess.

It was the first day back at school. To Maddie, it felt like forever since she and her twin sister, Mia, had spent time with their best friends. They charged across the blacktop and up the hill. Maddie would reach the tree last by a long shot for sure, but that didn't matter. Everything felt just how it had been before they left for Mom's summer concert tour—and that was saying something. Last night, she'd tossed and turned, waking up five or six times, worried. Annabeth and Emily's houses were just up the street from the Glimmers' house, and usually the girls saw each other almost every day. But would things be different now, after Maddie and her family had been gone nearly all summer?

"Come on, Maddie!" Mia shouted over her shoulder.

Maddie put on a burst of speed, gasping in a breath of crisp, cool air. The leaves of the giant oak tree had started to turn fiery red around their edges. Fall in Nashville was Maddie's favorite time of year.

"Guess what?" Mia said, at the exact moment Annabeth said the same thing.

"You first," Annabeth said.

Mia motioned for Maddie to tell.

Maddie fell to her knees in the grass beside her friends and said, "When we were in London, we caught an art thief."

"Actually, Maddie caught him," Mia added. "She snuck out all on her own—in London. Can you believe it?"

"And then Mia figured out who was letting animals out of their exhibits at Captain Swashbuckler's Adventure Park in San Diego," Maddie said.

"Two mysteries solved in one summer!" Mia gave Maddie a high five.

Annabeth and Emily exchanged a look. Maddie didn't know what the look meant, but her worries from last night rushed back into her mind.

"What did you want to tell us?" she asked.

At this, Annabeth's face lit up, making Maddie feel much, much better. Maybe the look didn't mean anything. Maybe her friends were just impatient to share their news.

Annabeth said, "We've been working on—"

Emily cut her off. "A dance! We've been working on it for most of the summer."

"Let's show them!" Annabeth leapt to her feet and shooed Emily away so they both had room to strike their poses.

"Ms. Carpenter even gave us special permission to use Emily's iPad during recess to play the music,"

Annabeth said. "We asked her this morning so we could surprise you!"

Emily tapped on the screen and found the song. As the beat began, Emily turned up the volume, then shoved the iPad into Maddie's hands. "Here, you can hold this."

"Perfect," Annabeth said, nodding to the music.

Maddie felt a pang. Maybe she was supposed to feel included because she was holding the iPad, but mostly, she felt left out. Had the girls left a part in the dance for her and Mia?

"Five, six, seven, eight!"

Maddie and Mia jumped back, narrowly missing getting knocked in the faces by the girls' swinging arms. Maddie watched the complicated pattern of steps. What struck her, more than the complicated moves her friends had clearly worked on for a long time, was how the dance was made for two. Only two. Their friends obviously hadn't planned to include Maddie and Mia when they came home.

"What do you think?" Annabeth asked breathlessly, as the song came to an end.

"Can you teach us?" Mia asked.

"Uh, well . . ." Annabeth stalled.

"It's kind of a dance for two," Emily said, and then added quickly, "because you guys were gone."

"Did you like it?" Annabeth asked.

"I'd like it better if there was something for Maddie and me to do, other than hold the music," Mia said.

"But it's a good dance," Maddie said, feeling the tension rise between her sister and their friends.

The trouble was, she agreed with Mia. It felt as though the girls had planned the dance without them on purpose. Annabeth and Emily didn't say anything, which felt worse than if they had argued.

"Do you want to try it again?" Annabeth asked Emily, as the silence started to feel uncomfortable. "The section with the turns wasn't quite right."

"Yeah, okay . . ." Emily looked at Maddie. "Could you play the song again?"

"Seriously?" Mia asked, looking from one of their friends to the other.

"It's okay, Mia," Maddie said. "I don't mind."

"Well, I have better things to do than stand here and watch you dance." Mia took off across the blacktop toward the school—probably to go to the library.

Maddie swallowed hard. Maybe their friends didn't know how left out they'd made her and Mia feel. But how couldn't they know? Mia had made her feelings pretty clear.

Annabeth stared after Mia and then shrugged. "You guys get to go all over the place on tour. And this is just a dance. You weren't here to make it with us. That's all. You understand, right, Maddie?"

"Yeah." Maddie tapped the screen to start the song over. "Yeah, I understand."

The girls launched into the dance again, and Maddie plastered a smile on her face. After five more run-throughs, the bell finally rang and they went back inside.

Fifth grade wasn't very different from fourth. Since they had the same teacher as they'd had last year, their subjects picked up right where they had left off. Today they focused on fractions, Latin, and writing out long passages of Shakespeare in cursive. In cursive, they practiced what Ms. Carpenter called the "lost art of handwriting." The second half of the day dragged on. All Maddie could hear in her head was Annabeth and Emily's song. Mia kept shooting her "Are you okay?" looks. The last hour of the day was so long, Maddie started counting how many times she looked up at the clock. Thirty-three by the time they were dismissed.

"See you tomorrow," Emily called to Maddie.

Maddie nodded, not trusting herself to speak. She stuffed her books into her bag and followed Mia out to the pick-up line to meet Lulu and wait for Miss Julia.

TWO

W e got to write stories today in class," Lulu called to her sisters, bubbling over with excitement. "And I wrote a mystery, kind of like the ones we solved this summer. But different."

"Hmm . . ." Mia said.

"What's your mystery about?" Maddie asked, since she could see that Mia was too full of held-back words to ask.

"A fairy and her magic dust. The magic dust gets stolen, and the fairy has to figure out who took it."

Miss Julia pulled up, and the girls climbed into the car.

The minute the doors shut, Mia's pent-up words burst out. "I can't believe them. And I can't believe you put up with it like that, Maddie."

"So, the fairy lives in a hole in a tree, like an owl," Lulu said, seeming not to notice Mia's outburst. "But she's tiny, so she can fit a hammock to sleep on in her house, and a little shelf for making food. Plus, she gathers rainwater for her teeny sink. And she collected cotton fluff from wish-flowers to make a soft couch. She keeps her fairy dust in a box she carved out of wood. So, one day after she's been flying around the forest with her fairy friend, she comes home and her fairy dust is gone!"

"Uh-oh," Maddie said.

"I know, and that's when the mystery starts." Lulu was so excited, she couldn't sit still. She kicked the seat in front of her. "Oops! Sorry, Miss Julia."

"Everyone buckled in?" Miss Julia asked.

"Yes," Maddie said.

"Yes," Mia grumbled.

"Umm . . ." Lulu said as she clicked her belt into place. "Okay. Yep, me too."

"They could have waited for us to come home to invent a dance," Mia said to no one in particular. "Or at least left room in their dance to add us when we got home."

Lulu kept telling her story, full-steam ahead. "The fairy thinks she sees a footprint, so she looks for more, but there aren't any. As you know, fairies fly, so they don't leave footprints. That's a problem. But since there aren't any footprints, she's pretty sure it must be a fairy. But, she's not sure how to find any more clues."

Mia continued, "I mean, we all take dance class together. It only makes sense for us to all be in the dance."

Maddie bounced between her sisters, trying to follow both conversations. The more Mia talked, the more Maddie's eyes and nose burned. She'd held in her hurt feelings all day long.

Lulu said, "But then, the fairy realizes there might be clues that aren't footprints. So, she starts to pay attention to anything out of the ordinary."

"It's like they meant to leave us out," Mia said.

Maddie blinked and blinked, but she couldn't hold the tears back anymore. They rolled down her cheeks. Lulu stopped midsentence, shocked into silence.

"Oh, Maddie, don't cry," Mia said.

"I'm just . . . it's just . . ." Maddie tried to put what she was feeling into words. On the tour this summer, so much had happened. She thought she'd moved beyond tears, but here they were spilling out, whether she wanted them to or not.

"I know what we can do," Mia said. "We can make up our own dance, you and me."

"And me!" Lulu added.

Mia's mouth tilted up in a half smile. "Okay, yes, and you too, Lulu. We can put on a show for Mom and Dad tonight like we sometimes do."

"And we can charge a quarter!" Lulu said.

"True," Mia said. "What do you say, Maddie?"

Maddie nodded. "I like that idea."

"Just in case anyone cares," Miss Julia said from the front seat, "I like the idea too. And I'll definitely pay a quarter to see your dance."

"I don't know why I'm crying," Maddie said.

"I do," Mia said. "Annabeth and Emily are acting like everything is different, just because we were gone for a few months."

"I don't want them to have moved on without us," Maddie said.

"Everything was different in my classroom too,"
Lulu said. "But different good. Last year, we only got to
write sentences. Now we get to write a whole story."

Maddie wiped her cheeks, and then wiped her
hands on her leggings. "Maybe we can show them our
dance tomorrow."

"And we won't let them be in ours, either," Mia said.

"Well, maybe we should . . ." Maddie said.

Mia raised an eyebrow.

"We can decide later," Maddie said quickly, and
turned to Lulu. "So, does she solve the mystery?"

Lulu frowned. "Who?"

"Your fairy."

"Oh!" Lulu said. "Yes! She sees toad footprints
outside her house, and figures her fairy dust was
kidnapped—"

"You can't kidnap dust," Mia pointed out.

"Well, it's stolen, then." Lulu said. "Stolen by the
toad. But fairy dust doesn't work on toads. It makes him
sick to his stomach when he tries to eat it. So, the fairy
finds the toad by the pond, looking greener than usual.
He has all her dust in his backpack."

"And he gives it back to her?" Maddie asked.

"Doesn't that seem too easy?" Mia asked.

"Sometimes things work out easier than you think,"
Lulu said.

Mia elbowed Maddie. "About that, she's right. This
dance thing will be okay too."

"Our dance will be more than okay," Maddie said, realizing she believed this just as she said it.

"It will be fantabulous!" Lulu said as they pulled into their driveway. "Glimmer girls sparkle and shine . . ."

"But most of all, they are kind," said her sisters, and even Miss Julia chimed in.

THREE

L ike this, Mia," Lulu insisted, repeating the complicated jump-twirl move, nearly toppling over onto Mia's bedroom floor.

Mia flopped onto her bed. "I'm not doing that, Lulu."

"But we want the dance to be fantabulous!" Lulu said. "Come on, please, Mia?"

Maddie perched on the edge of Mia's bed, hoping a plan would spring to mind. She knew it wouldn't help to point out that no one could do the jump-twirl Lulu had suggested the same way twice . . . not even Lulu. Lulu would argue, and Mia would insist she could do the move, she just didn't want to.

"How about this?" Maddie suggested, jumping up to demonstrate. She spun once and then landed on one knee, arms raised.

Lulu's bottom lip jutted out as she faced off with Mia.

"Or this?" Maddie tried another spin, this time ending with jazz hands.

"You're doing the same thing over and over," Lulu said. "Just with different hands."

"This isn't working," Mia said.

"Dinner in ten minutes!" Mom called from downstairs.

Lulu jumped to her feet, eyes wild. "Dinner in ten minutes! We need an end, we need an end!"

"What if we do the dance exactly as we've planned it—together—and on that last beat, we can each do a move we like best," Maddie said.

Mia tilted her head, thinking. "That's actually a good idea. Nice one, Maddie."

"Start the music!" Lulu shouted, posing in the middle of the room.

Maddie leapt up and started the music before anyone could say anything else. As the beat began, they danced through the routine they'd created. Just as Maddie had known would happen, frowns turned to smiles. The rhythm of the music made Maddie's heart race as they stepped and turned and twirled. She challenged herself to extend her arms fully and keep every step right in time with the beat. Right and left and right again, and then the wave starting with Mia, followed by Lulu and finishing up with Maddie. As the music ended, they each added their own flair-filled last move and struck final poses.

"And then, applause!" Lulu dipped into a low curtsy.

Maddie and Mia curtsied too, and the girls gave each other high fives.

"We did it!" Mia said.

"And I get to do the twirl-kick!" Lulu did her signature move one more time.

Mia shook her head, but this time she was smiling.

"Girls, come on down for dinner," Mom called again.

Maddie followed her sisters downstairs, starved after all the dancing. They each took their seats around the dining table and bowed their heads to pray.

"God, bless this food to our bodies, and help us to bless others in all we say and do," Dad prayed.

"Amen," they all chimed in.

Dinner was tomato soup with crusty bread and a salad. Lulu resisted the salad, but in the end, she decided the dressing made the lettuce taste all right. Maddie agreed. She liked the tangy dressing with the hint of salt from the crunchy almonds scattered on top.

"May we be dismissed?" Mia asked, the minute her plate was clear.

Mom checked their plates. "You may. Miss Julia said she'd be back for the show at seven. Do you think you'll be ready about then?"

"Will we ever!" Lulu said, bounding toward the stairs.

"Don't forget, the show costs a quarter," Maddie said.

"Oh, I'm already ready." Dad pulled his quarter out of his pocket. "Can't wait!"

Once they were upstairs, Maddie went straight to her closet to figure out her costume.

Maddie called to her sisters, "So we're wearing leggings and shirts with sparkles, right?"

"Yes. You wear your purple one with the star." Lulu popped into Maddie's room from next door. "And I'll wear my pink tank top with sequins . . ."

"What are you going to wear, Mia?" Maddie called through the wall to her sister's room.

"My aqua shirt with the sparkly heart," Mia called back.

"And a sparkly headband!" Lulu said, already on her way to her room.

Maddie pulled on her outfit and added a sequin star barrette to match. Mia and Lulu burst through the door, and they all lined up in front of Maddie's full-length mirror.

"Perfect," Maddie said. She loved the way their bright colors matched without being exactly the same.

"I think I heard Miss Julia come in," Lulu said.

"I'll go down and set up the music," Mia said. "Maddie can set up the seats, and Lulu can collect quarters."

"And keep them?" Lulu asked.

"We'll each get one," Mia said. "That way it's fair."

"Good thing we have three people in our audience," Maddie said.

"True," Mia agreed. "Are we ready?"

"Ready!" Lulu said.

They nearly tumbled over one another in their rush to be first downstairs. Mom, Dad, and Miss Julia were already on the couch, so Maddie didn't need to set up

chairs. Lulu turned her cowboy hat upside down to collect quarters. Mia cued up the music.

"Okay, everyone close your eyes," Mia said. "You
can open them when the music starts."

She hurried to join her sisters, and posed in the few
seconds before the beat began. Mom and Dad opened
their eyes and leaned forward to watch. Miss Julia
took out her phone and snapped photo after photo. The
dance went even better than it had during rehearsal.
When the music finished and the girls posed, the
grown-ups leapt to their feet to applaud.

"Girls, I'm so impressed. You were right in time with
each other," Mom said. "And I'm glad you were able to
do the show tonight. Remember, the rest of this week,
Dad and I are going to be busy every night."

"For the benefit," Maddie said, remembering. With
everything that had happened in school that day, and
the rush of just arriving home from tour, the benefit
for Third Street Community House had been far from
her mind. But, she'd been thinking about the benefit concert a lot this summer. She and her sisters had
been practicing their own version of "This Little Light
of Mine," and Mom planned to let them sing in a show
sometime soon. Would the benefit be the right time for
their performance?

It was one of those moments when Mia seemed to
read Maddie's mind, because she said, "Are we singing
in the benefit?"

"I've been thinking about it," Mom said. "Let me talk it over with Dad, and we'll decide in the next couple days."

"Please, please, pretty please?" Lulu pleaded. "With whipped cream and a cherry on top?"

Mom smiled, but didn't give any more hints about what she was thinking. "Now, girls, I bet you have some homework that isn't done yet, since you've danced the afternoon away. Is that true?"

"Yes," Mia and Maddie said together.

Lulu sighed. "I don't have any homework."

"You're lucky you don't have homework yet," Mia said.

"Hmph," Lulu said, clearly not agreeing.

Mia shrugged. "Well, if you really want homework, maybe you can write another story about your fairy."

Lulu's face lit up. "I wrote a mystery about a fairy!" she explained to Mom and Dad, and then launched into the full story for them.

Maddie passed a quarter to Mia and took one for herself, leaving the third in the hat for Lulu. "Hey, Mia, first one to write out the whole passage of Shakespeare gets to tell Annabeth and Emily about our dance!"

Mia stuck out her hand to shake. "Deal."

The minute they let go of hands, Maddie took off running. Mia stayed on her heels all the way upstairs.

FOUR

Even though she was supposed to do her cursive homework at her desk, Maddie flopped on her bed to copy out the Shakespeare passage. As long as the work got finished, did it really matter where she sat? Maddie paused, midsentence, thinking this through. She'd never lied to Ms. Carpenter about where she'd done her homework, but it wasn't exactly truthful to leave out the details. Maddie considered moving to her desk, but before she could decide, the doorbell rang.

"Who's that?" Maddie called through the wall to Mia.

The doorbell didn't often ring this late in the evening, and if it did, it was always someone they were expecting.

"No idea," Mia called back.

Maddie tried to stay focused, carefully writing the next word in the passage, which happened to be *misery*. Laughter and voices drifted upstairs.

"Whoever it is, we know them," Maddie said. "Come on, Mia, aren't you curious?"

No answer.

Maddie tossed her pen down on her notebook. "Well, I'm going to go find out who it is."

She bounded downstairs, and she wasn't surprised when Mia followed closely after. Mia never liked being the last to know anything.

Lulu was already downstairs. "Look, it's Ms. Carpenter!"

"Hi, girls," Ms. Carpenter said.

Maddie stopped short. "I'm sorry, I didn't mean to be doing my homework on my bed!"

Ms. Carpenter and Mom gave Maddie a quizzical look. Mia raised an eyebrow too, but her look wasn't so much "huh?" as it was "really, Maddie?"

Maddie looked from Mia to Ms. Carpenter and back again. "Umm . . . are you here to check on us . . . about our homework?"

Ms. Carpenter and Mom both looked like they were about to laugh, but Maddie didn't see what was so funny. That's when she noticed Ms. Carpenter's guitar case.

"Ms. Carpenter is giving Mom a guitar!" Lulu said.

"For the Third Street Benefit," Mom explained. "Actually, it's a particularly special guitar, girls." She glanced at Ms. Carpenter. "Should we show them?"

Ms. Carpenter's face lit up. "Let's!"

"We can set it right here." Mom cleared space on the dining table.

"Oh, hi there, Jennifer," Dad said, coming in from the kitchen.

"Jennifer brought us Earl Eldridge Jr.'s guitar for the silent auction," Mom said.

"That's right, he was your great-grandfather, wasn't he?" Dad asked. "What a generous gift."

"We have a lot of memorabilia from his performing days, enough to fill at least one whole room," Ms. Carpenter said. "It doesn't seem right to have the guitar sitting around gathering dust when it could be helping people instead."

She opened the case and lifted out a battered-looking guitar.

Dad ran his hand over the worn wood. "Amazing."

Now, Ms. Carpenter did burst out laughing. "Not what you expected, Maddie?"

Maddie realized she must have been making a face. "Oh, no, it looks . . . I mean . . ."

"Earl Eldridge played this guitar for over forty years," Dad said. "Of course, he could have replaced it many times over, but he called this one his Old Faithful."

"Grandpa and his guitar were inseparable," Ms. Carpenter said.

"And you're sure you want to donate it?" Dad asked.

"I'm hoping that whomever wins it in the auction won't leave it on a shelf. Guitars shouldn't stay silent," Ms. Carpenter said. "That's what Grandpa always said. I held on to the guitar for longer than I should have, but I was waiting for an opportunity that felt just right. And then I heard about your benefit, Gloria. Back in the day, Grandpa Earl served at a soup kitchen every month. I know he'd want to support your cause."

"What's a soup kitchen?" Lulu wanted to know.

"A soup kitchen is a place where nutritious, hot food is served to people who are hungry," Mom said. "Volunteers cook and serve the food. You girls and I are actually volunteering at the Third Street Community House soup kitchen this week, on Thursday. Not every shelter has a soup kitchen for the public, but Third Street does. That's one of the things I like most about Third Street. As soon as residents check in, they are given jobs to do at the shelter. Everyone helps out, serving one another and the greater community. Part of the money we raise at the benefit will help Third Street buy food for the soup kitchen. It will also help to buy warm clothes and shoes for shelter residents and others who need them. We're also supporting the shelter itself, where people who don't have homes can stay temporarily while they work toward finding a job and a place to live."

"But why don't they have homes?" Lulu asked.

Sometimes when they drove around the city, Maddie saw tents or even cardboard boxes under bridges. She had a hard time believing people actually lived in those places, out in the cold, but she knew it was true. It made her sad to see people who didn't have warm coats or good shoes, people who clearly didn't have enough money to buy the things they needed.

Dad thought for a moment about Lulu's question and then said, "When you don't have a place to live, it's hard to get a job. Once you're homeless, it's a hard problem to fix. That's why Third Street is so important to the community, and why we're committed to raising money to support their work."

"So you think auctioning the guitar could make a lot of money?" Mia asked, eyeing the battered instrument doubtfully.

"It's worn out, but with lots of love," Mom said.

Ms. Carpenter turned the guitar on its side. "And see here, there's a chip at the base of the guitar. In one of his concerts, Grandpa's shoulder strap was so frayed that it broke and he dropped the guitar. The guitar was okay—aside from the chip—but he had to replace the strap."

"So, that's how you know it's not just any guitar?" Maddie asked.

"Exactly," Ms. Carpenter answered. "I hear you girls are going to the Opry this week too. Maybe when you're there, you can see pictures of Earl Eldridge Jr. and hear more stories about him. He was one of the most famous singers in Nashville back when the Opry was founded, almost 90 years ago."

"Whoa!" Lulu said. "That's a long time."

Ms. Carpenter gave Maddie her teacher look. "So, are you going to go finish up that homework at your desk?"

Maddie crinkled her nose. "Yes."

"I will too," Mia said.

"And I'll sit at my desk to write my story!" Lulu said.

Ms. Carpenter smiled. "Okay, then. See you tomor-row, girls."

"Bye!" The girls waved good-bye.

After she closed the door behind Ms. Carpenter, Mom said, "To your desks!" and chased them all back upstairs.

FIVE

So, we'll show Annabeth and Emily the dance at morning recess." Mia buckled her seat belt, ready for the ride to school.

Maddie decided not to point out that Mia had already mentioned this six times this morning. "Sounds good."

"But I don't have the same morning recess!" Lulu wailed. As usual, Lulu was in her booster seat, with Maddie wedged into the middle seat between her sisters. "You can't do the dance without me!"

"We don't need—" Mia began.

"We'll do the dance with you later, Lulu," Maddie said. "And we'll tell the girls you helped us create it." Technically, it was true that they didn't need Lulu to do the dance, but telling her so wouldn't make for a happy drive.

"Please, please, please . . . Invite Annabeth and Emily over this afternoon. We can show them together," Lulu said.

"But Mom said we're going to the Grand Ole Opry tonight to help with the auction items," Mia said. "And what are we supposed to do at recess, watch Annabeth and Emily dance the whole time? This way, we can have a dance-off."

"Ooh!" Maddie clapped her hands. "A dance-off!"

"And maybe we can have someone judge which of the dances is best!" Mia said. "We'll definitely win."

Miss Julia pulled up to the curb at school, but before she unlocked the doors, she turned in her seat to look at them, her expression serious. "Girls, are you sure you want to compete with your friends? Remember how hurt your feelings were yesterday."

"It will be a fun competition." Mia threw open her door. "Friendly competition."

Maddie pulled her backpack over her shoulder and followed Mia out of the car. Now that Miss Julia brought it up, she wasn't so sure a dance-off was the best idea. The whole reason she and Mia had made the dance was to keep from feeling left out. Or actually, to stop any more distance from opening up between them and their friends. What if a dance-off made the gap even wider?

"Have a nice day at school, girls," Miss Julia said, still with a hesitant tone in her voice.

"Bye, Miss Julia," Lulu said, climbing out to join her sisters.

"See you this afternoon!" Maddie said.

"Bye!" Mia called, closing the door.

As soon as they were through the school's front door, Lulu ran off to join her friend, Sara. At least for the time being, she'd completely forgotten about the dance.

"Hey, there's Annabeth and Emily!" Mia said, and then called to their friends. "Annabeth! Emily! We made a dance last night. We can have a dance-off at morning recess!"

Annabeth and Emily exchanged another of their looks as they crossed the entryway to where Mia and Maddie stood. Maddie didn't like the silent language that had sprung up between her friends, especially since she could only guess at what it meant. Nothing good, as far as she could tell.

Annabeth shrugged. "Sure. Who will judge it?"

"Maybe we can ask Ms. Carpenter." Mia stood on her tiptoes to see if she could spot their teacher.

"Sure, if she will," Emily said.

"Ms. Carpenter came to our house last night," Mia continued, not seeming to notice the tension. "Did you know her great-grandfather was Earl Eldridge Jr.?"

"Who's that?" Annabeth asked.

"You don't know?" Mia's face lit up, clearly excited to share what she'd learned last night. "Only the grandfather of country music! Ms. Carpenter donated his guitar for the silent auction at the Third Street Benefit this weekend. Oh!" She stopped in her tracks. "You guys are still coming to the show, right? Mom said she set aside tickets for you. But it's even better than a normal concert, because Maddie, Lulu, and I are probably going to sing! At the Opry!"

Annabeth raised an eyebrow at Emily, and the knot in Maddie's stomach twisted tighter. This wasn't going well, and Mia hadn't seemed to notice. Before Maddie

could figure out what to do, they'd reached their classroom door.

"Good morning, girls," Ms. Carpenter called.
"Hurry to your seats. We have a lot to cover today." As
Maddie and Mia sat down, she asked, "And how did the
rest of that handwriting homework go last night?"

"We sat at our desks!" Mia said. "Well, at least
I did."

Maddie was only half paying attention. She was
too busy watching Annabeth and Emily. They'd leaned
their heads toward one another and were whispering
back and forth. Every once in a while, one of them
would glance up at Maddie or Mia. Maddie tried to
look away whenever this happened, so she wouldn't be
caught staring. Still, she was pretty sure they caught her
at least once.

The morning sped by. Ms. Carpenter had paperwork
she needed to finish at her desk during recess, and
no one wanted to ask Mr. Shelton, their PE teacher, to
judge the dance-off. So, at least for today, there wouldn't
be a competition.

"Still, we want to show you our dance," Mia said.
"Race you to the tree!"

They ran their usual route across the blacktop and
over to a grassy patch by the oak tree. Mia started
the music. Maddie knew her sister was on a mission
to help her feel better. Mia thought that if their dance
could be as good—or better—compared to Annabeth

and Emily's, then things would go back to normal. But, from the way Annabeth and Emily were acting, Maddie knew that showing them up wouldn't help at all.

"Five, six, seven, eight!" Mia called out as the music began.

Maddie tried not to look at Annabeth and Emily, and instead let the music take over. Even more than when she sang, when Maddie danced, she totally lost herself in the music and movement. After all the worries of the morning, it was a relief to let go and stop thinking about everyone else. They made it to the final pose, out of breath and grinning.

Mia gave Maddie a high five. "That's what I'm talking about!"

"Great job." Emily shoved her hands into her pockets and looked at her shoes.

"We should go work on our dance," Annabeth said to Emily, avoiding eye contact with Mia and Maddie.

"Is something wrong?" Mia tried to catch Annabeth's eye, and then Emily's, but neither looked back at her. "Your dance is already great. You don't have to work on—"

"You don't know everything," Annabeth snapped. "And just because we didn't spend the summer on tour or get invited to sing at the Opry, doesn't mean we couldn't do those things."

"Annabeth . . ." Emily threw Maddie a concerned glance.

"We watched your dance, and now we'd like to go work on ours," Annabeth said. "Right, Emily?"

Emily dug her toe into the grass. "Yeah, I guess."

"Why are they so mad?" Mia asked, watching them walk away.

Maddie sank to the ground and leaned her back against the tree. All she wanted was for things to go back to the way they were. But, the more she tried to hold on to the way things used to be, the more everything changed.

"Don't worry." Mia sat next to her sister and wrapped her arm around Maddie's shoulders. "All of this—whatever it is—will blow over soon."

"I hope so," Maddie said, meaning it.

SIX

Lulu wriggled in her booster seat. "How long until we get there?"

Mom checked the girls out in the rearview mirror. "Just a minute or two more."

From the passenger seat, Miss Julia turned to look at them too. "Anyone need anything? I packed a picnic dinner to eat backstage a little later, but do you need anything now? Snack bar or anything?"

"No, thank you," they all answered.

Mom followed Dad, caravan style. They needed both cars since they'd brought so many auction items. Plus, some of the band members had squeezed into the car with Dad. Maddie watched out the window as they wound through side streets on the outskirts of Nashville. Outside, the wind was blowing hard, whipping tree branches back and forth with wild gusts.

"Why again is the Opry so far away from town?" Maddie knew that if no one had an answer, Miss Julia would find out and teach them all something new.

"It used to be some kind of farm." Miss Julia tapped her phone to find the details, just like Maddie guessed she would. "Right. It was farmland used for making sausages."

"How does a farm make—" Lulu started.

Mia cut her off. "Don't ask."

Lulu gave Mia a puzzled look.

Miss Julia shrugged. "Sausage comes from pigs."

"Oh," Lulu said, and then made a face. "Right."

"So, the Grand Ole Opry started at the National Life & Accident Insurance's radio venue," Miss Julia explained. "More and more fans wanted to see the country music show, and they kept outgrowing their space. They ended up at the Ryman Auditorium downtown. The Ryman stuck for a while, but then they wanted an even larger space—one with air conditioning and plenty of parking. So, in 1974, they built the theater out here."

"There's plenty of parking," Mia pointed out, as they passed through the mall's giant parking lot.

"Before the new Opry building opened, they opened a theme park out here, called Opryland."

"With rides?" Lulu wanted to know.

Miss Julia consulted her phone. "There were some rides. One was called Flume Zoom. Later on, it was renamed Dulcimer Splash. They also had the Timber Topper, which became the Rock and Roller Coaster."

"Ooh, like the barrel ride this summer," Lulu said. "Remember when Mia saw that seal in the water, Maddie?"

"On Barrel Buffoonery," Maddie said. "That was one of my favorite rides in the whole park."

"My favorite thing at the park were the Belgian waffles," Lulu said. "Oooh. Are we going to have popcorn at the Opry tonight?"

"Remember, it's not a regular night at the Opry. We'll be getting ready for the auction," Mom said. "We need to tag all the auction items and see what we're still missing."

"What kinds of things will there be?" Mia asked. "More guitars?"

Mom said, "There are a few instruments. A banjo, an accordion, some harmonicas, a couple ukuleles, and a tuba. There are also some gift baskets with concert tickets and gift certificates for dinner or dessert. People like to bid on experiences, so we have a couple baskets that offer dinner with famous musicians."

"Like Beethoven?" Lulu asked.

"Taylor Swift?" Maddie asked.

"Or the Glimmer Girls," said Mia. "Since we're having our Grand Ole Opry debut!"

"We'll see about that," Mom said.

Dad pulled up near the loading dock, and parked next to the other members of the band. Everyone piled out of the cars. The band grabbed their instruments, and the Glimmers filled their arms with auction items. Maddie ended up with a giant basket stuffed so full of tissue paper, she could barely see over the top. The loading dock door was open, so she headed in that general direction.

She was so busy trying to navigate the parking lot, she nearly ran right into a man wearing jeans with holes in the knees. He had a scruffy beard, and hair that poked out from under a blue-and-maroon-striped wool cap. Surprised, Maddie stepped back and edged closer to Miss Julia.

"That's a lot of guitars you have there . . . Need me to take one of those off your hands?" he called after the band, his voice a little louder than it needed to be.

"Who is he?" Maddie whispered to Miss Julia, hoping the man couldn't hear.

"Don't worry," Miss Julia answered, putting her arm around Maddie. "You're safe."

"Not this afternoon," Dad answered the man, smiling apologetically.

"Never hurts to ask." When the man smiled at Dad, it was like the sun had come out from behind clouds. His eyes lit up and, for just a moment, he looked kind and gentle and like he'd be easy to talk to.

Maddie stayed close to Miss Julia, but she couldn't help thinking this man, whoever he was, didn't seem quite as bad as she'd thought at first.

"Do you think he's homeless?" Mia asked, once they were inside. "I mean, is he one of the people we're raising money to help?"

"I don't know." Maddie realized Mia might be right. The man had all the telltale signs. Dirty clothes, worn-out shoes, no coat—and that ragged wool hat. He was bony and thin, and looked like he might be hungry.

"Do you think a homeless person would smile like that?" she asked Mia. "I mean, he seemed . . . I don't know . . ."

"What'cha talking about?" Lulu asked, joining them. "And where do I put this thing down? Why do we need a gigantic basket for this tiny envelope?"

"This way, ladies." Miss Julia led them toward a room with wide-open doors, directly across the entry-way from the loading dock. The room had rows of pipes across the ceiling, with lots of theater lights.

"Is this a theater?" Maddie asked, looking around the room for a stage.

"It's a filming studio," Dad said. "This is where they filmed *Hee Haw*."

"What's that?" Lulu asked.

Dad grinned. "We'll have to show you sometime. You'd love the television show. It's an old-time musical revue with stories and singers. Lots of fun."

Tables had been set up around the room. The auction items were all clumped together on the middle table.

"Set your baskets here," Mom instructed. "Once we see what we have, we can spread them out across the tables. We'll stage the auction here, and on the night of the benefit, take everything out into the lobby so people can bid."

SEVEN

At first, shuttling the baskets to the various tables was a lot of fun. Dad let them oil the ukulele strings and polish the harmonicas. Lulu tried to play the banjo, but as the twangy music filled the room, Mom drew the line.

"Let's save music for the stage, girls. There's a lot to go through here, and we all need to be able to hear ourselves think."

"Can we go play the instruments on stage?" Lulu asked, but all the girls knew the answer to that question.

Unless the band members were supervising, no playing the instruments.

"Can we go look at the dressing rooms?" Mia asked Mom, acting a little restless now that their part of the work was done.

Maddie felt restless too. Now that they'd finished polishing instruments, there wasn't much to do. Watching Mom and the committee check paperwork wasn't all that interesting.

"Ooh!" Lulu said. "I want to come."

"I'll go with them," Miss Julia offered.

"Thanks, Julia," Mom said.

The dressing rooms were around the corner, through some double glass doors, and past the security desk. The girls and Miss Julia signed the clipboard and hung visitor badges around their necks.

"I'm Charles," the security guard told them, shaking each of their hands. "If you need anything, let me know. A couple of our staff are cleaning up the rooms. You never know, you might even be able to pry a story or two out of them."

"What are all those boxes?" Lulu asked.

To the right of the wood-paneled security desk, boxes with numbered glass doors lined a wall.

"Those are mailboxes for the current Opry members," Charles said. "Fan mail comes in for them from all across the country."

"Over here, they post all the members' names." Miss Julia pointed out the brass plaques that filled the wall behind them.

Maddie scanned the names. A lot of them she'd heard before, but she didn't know much of their music. "Carrie Underwood!" she said.

"Did your mom ever show you the video of her invitation to the Opry?" Miss Julia asked.

"No," the girls said.

Miss Julia pulled out her phone. "You have to see this. You girls will love it."

"Why don't you go on into the Women of Country Music dressing room?" Charles suggested. "Perfect place to watch that video."

"True," Miss Julia said. "Thank you!"

Framed photos and glass cases lined the back-stage hallway. Most of the pictures were of performers onstage. A glass case tucked into one of the walls was lit up and filled with costume pieces—a pearl-studded jacket, a shirt embroidered with holly and ivy, and some fancy boots. Information cards sat next to the items, explaining who had worn them and in which decade, making the hallway feel a little like a museum. Each dressing room had a sign on its door, and a specific name. They passed the Stars and Stripes Room, which had striped walls and flag pillows. A lighted mirror filled the far wall. Farther down the hallway, they found the Women of Country Music room. Maddie liked the curved blue couch and the soft brown and beige pillows that invited you to curl up and relax.

They squished together on the couch so everyone could see Miss Julia's phone. In the video, Carrie Underwood was just finishing a song on stage when she turned to see a man right beside her. Surprised, she shrieked and covered her mouth, and then gave him a big hug.

"Who is that man?" Maddie asked.

"That's Randy Travis," Miss Julia said.

He invited Carrie Underwood to become a member of the Opry. This was clearly a big deal. She pressed her hands to her face and looked ready to cry—happy tears. They watched all the way to the end, and then her interview after.

"It's a big deal, when you're invited to be an Opry member, isn't it?" Mia asked.

"It's a huge honor—you're being invited into a big, musical family," Miss Julia said.

"I want to be a member someday," Lulu announced.

"I can see that happening," Miss Julia said.

"And then I could wear sparkly costumes and have my own fan mail box!" Lulu said, bouncing off the couch and spinning around the room.

"There's a lot of work involved too," Miss Julia said. "Opry members have to earn their membership all through their careers. They work hard, and pay dues too."

Lulu wasn't really listening. She was too busy dancing around and imagining herself on stage.

"Can we go look at some of the other rooms?" Mia asked.

"Sure," said Miss Julia. "Lead the way, girls."

They wandered from room to room. Each one had a lighted mirror and some kind of couch or cushy chairs, and pictures of singers who'd been at the Opry over the years. To Maddie, the dressing rooms felt alive with stories from the past, and made her feel that if you spent much time here, the talent—and courage—of all those past singers might just rub off on you.

"Do you think Mom will let us sing on Friday?" Mia asked, as they came into the Cousin Minnie room, which was blue and pink, and even had an upright piano in it.

"I don't know." Maddie still couldn't picture herself standing on that stage, in front of an audience filled with people, singing. Not even if her sisters were up there with her. The thought of it made a whole flock of butterflies flutter in circles inside her stomach.

Lulu led everyone into a room around the corner, where they found a woman straightening the chairs and dusting off the small end tables.

"Well, hello there," she said to the girls. "Welcome to the greenroom!"

"Why is it called the greenroom?" Lulu asked.

"All theaters have a greenroom," Mia said. "Where the singers or actors wait for the show."

"Aren't their dressing rooms for that?" Lulu asked.

"Sometimes they want to be with the other performers, and the greenroom is a good place to gather," the woman said. "The reason why they call the performers' waiting room a greenroom is lost to history. Some people think it's because one of the first waiting rooms for performers was painted green. But no one knows for sure. By the way, I'm Amanda."

"I'm Mia," Mia said. "This is Maddie, and that's Lulu."

"Hi there," Miss Julia said, holding out her hand to shake Amanda's. "I'm Julia."

"So, you're getting ready for Friday's benefit," Amanda said to the girls.

"Mom is setting up the auction items," Lulu said. "And we're learning our way around backstage, so we'll be ready. We're going to sing!"

"We might sing," Mia corrected.

"Mom's going to let us," Lulu said confidently, causing Maddie's butterflies to flutter all over again.

"We'll see," Miss Julia said. "Actually, Amanda, the girls were hoping we'd find someone backstage who knew some of the Opry's history. Mia and Maddie's teacher, Jennifer Carpenter, is the great-granddaughter of Earl Eldridge Jr. She donated his guitar for the benefit."

"I have some excellent stories about Earl Eldridge Jr.," Amanda said. "Want to sit a while?"

EIGHT

A ctually, before you sit," Amanda said, "come on over here and take a look at this picture. Here's the man himself, and I'm willing to bet this guitar he's holding is the one you're auctioning."

Maddie squinted at the black-and-white picture, looking for the telltale chip. "It might be. I can't see the chip at this angle."

"He dropped the guitar one night," Lulu said, "when his strap broke, and the guitar got chipped. But even then, he didn't want a new guitar. He thought the chip made his old guitar even more beautiful."

Amanda nodded, smiling. "That's right. Sounds like you girls are already experts."

"Why was he so famous, though?" Mia wanted to know. "Was it just because he was one of the first members of the Opry?"

"That's not the only reason," Amanda said, gesturing to the couches.

The girls squeezed onto a couch that was a lot smaller than the blue one in the Women of Country Music room. Miss Julia sat in a chair next to them. Amanda leaned forward, elbows on her knees, her eyes sparkling. Before she even got started, Maddie could see she loved telling stories.

"It all began on the night of November 28, 1925, with a radio broadcast hosted by George D. Hay. He called his show a one-hour barn dance, and it was full of old-time fiddle music and fun. People kept tuning in week after week. In 1927, for the first time, the words 'Grand Ole Opry' were broadcast across the radio. Soon, they added a live audience. From there, the show grew and grew, outgrowing its space time and again. In fact, the show's popularity is one of the main reasons that people started calling Nashville 'Music City.'"

"But what about Earl Eldridge Jr.?" Lulu asked.

"He was quite something," Amanda said. "He was known for his chin whiskers and gold teeth—you saw those in the picture. E. E. Jr. would hoot and holler and stomp in the recording studio, giving the technicians a terrible time as they tried to manage the sound levels."

"E. E. Jr.?" Maddie asked.

"Yes, that's what people called him. He was a comedian as well as a musician, and everyone said his tales were the tallest of them all. One time, he tried to convince the Opry listeners that he'd been swallowed by a whale, just like Jonah."

"No one believed it, though," Mia said. "Right?

"As many times as he told that one, people started to wonder," Amanda said, laughing. "I've heard some old recordings where he'd spin that yarn, moaning over the smell inside the whale's belly, and explaining all the ways he tried to come up, with no escape."

"So how'd he finally escape?" Lulu asked.

Mia elbowed her sister. "Lulu, he wasn't actually swallowed by a whale."

Lulu elbowed Mia right back. "Well, how did he say he got out, anyway?"

"It was a different story each time," Amanda said. "My favorite—of the ones I've heard—is that a starfish tickled the whale's insides so fiercely that the whale coughed them both up."

"Ms. Carpenter said he served at a soup kitchen a lot," Maddie said.

"True. People who didn't have enough to eat would line up, and there E. E. Jr. would be, telling jokes, dishing up soup, grinning his gold-toothed smile. I hear he used to say it wasn't much good to warm up a person's belly if you didn't warm up his heart too."

"I wish I could have met him," Mia said. "He sounds like a fun person."

"Me too," Maddie said. "I'm glad we heard these stories about him. They make the guitar even more special."

"It will certainly be a special item for the fortunate person who wins it in the auction," Amanda said.

"Speaking of which," Miss Julia said. "Girls, we should probably check in on how things are going in the studio. Are you ready to head back?"

"I wanted to see the stage, though!" Lulu said.

"It's okay with me if the girls want to go on through to the stage and take a look," Amanda said. "As long as they don't touch any of the rigging or other equipment. But it's fun to see the stage, especially when it's quiet and empty the way it is right now."

"We promise not to touch any instruments," Mia said. "Plus, some of the band members might even be out there still, setting up. Please, Miss Julia?"

"As long as you promise to be on your best behavior. And no more than fifteen minutes. Then, if I haven't come to get you, I want you to head straight back to the studio."

"Got it," Mia said.

"We promise," Maddie said.

"Lulu?" Miss Julia gave Lulu a look that meant business.

"Cross my heart, promise," she said.

"And I'll be right here, girls," Amanda said. "If you need anything at all."

"Let's go!" Mia jumped to her feet.

"To your right," Amanda called after them, laughing.

Even though Mom, Dad, and Miss Julia were just a few rooms away, it seemed too good to be true to go through the stage doors, into the darkened theater wings, and past the curtains onto the stage all on their own.

"Whoa!" Lulu said.

"Whoa is right," Mia said, eyes wide.

NINE

Beyond the stage, rows of seats seemed to go on and on and on. The guitars, drums, and keyboard had been set up, and the band members were gone. There it was—the Grand Ole Opry stage, completely empty, with a microphone waiting. It was too much for Lulu. She rushed over, reached up to tap the microphone—which thankfully wasn't on, and was far above her head, anyway—and launched into song.

"You are my sunshine, my only sunshine . . ." Lulu sang.

"Lulu!" Mia hurried over to her, stopping just short of the circle of worn wood under Lulu's feet. "You're standing in the circle."

Lulu looked down and shrugged. "No one was using it."

"Lulu, the Opry circle is special," Mia said. "Do you know how many singers have stood there and performed?"

"Do you?" Lulu shot back. "I don't know, probably lots."

"They cut the wood out of the Ryman Auditorium floor and brought it here," Mia said. "And just about every country singer you can think of has stood on this stage—either here at this auditorium or there at the Ryman."

"I know," Lulu said, even though Maddie was pretty sure she didn't.

"So, shouldn't you save standing on it for your real Opry debut?" Mia pressed.

"I'm sure we'll stand here tons of times this week," Lulu said. "Mom's going to make us practice if we're going to sing for real."

Maddie looked out at the empty seats and the rows of lights shining along the underside of the balcony. Lulu's words bounced around in Maddie's head. *If we're going to sing for real.* Would they? And if they did, how many people would be sitting up there, staring at them? If even half the seats were full, that would be far too many eyes staring at Maddie.

"How many people does the theater hold?" Mia asked, yet again seeming to read Maddie's mind.

"No idea." Maddie looked for a place to sit down, suddenly not feeling so well.

"Lots and lots!" Lulu said. "But it's not as big as some concert halls."

"It's big enough," Mia said. "Bigger than anywhere we've ever sung before. Plus, it's the Opry—our very first concert at the Opry!"

Maddie finally decided to sit on a speaker. It was the only thing she could find, and her legs were so wobbly by then that if she didn't sit, she might topple over.

"You okay?" Mia gave her a concerned glance. "You don't look so great."

"She's scared about all those people," Lulu said, and then started singing again. "You make me happy when skies are gray."

"Lulu," Mia said. "Come on, please get off the circle. Honestly, before we get in trouble."

"We won't get in trouble," Lulu said. "No one is here. Come on, Mia. You know you want to sing too."

Mia's mouth quirked up in a half smile. "Actually, Lulu is right, Maddie. We can sing right now with no one to hear us. Come on, it will be fun."

Maddie glanced over into the wings. Mia was right. With Miss Julia checking in with Mom, and everyone else busy with the auction items, the only person who might hear them was Amanda. And she was a few rooms away. If she truly was going to sing on Friday night—which she still couldn't picture—she should try to warm herself up to the idea.

She stood, testing her watery legs. They weren't much steadier than before. Mia didn't wait for Maddie to change her mind. Instead, she grabbed her arm and yanked her over to the edge of the circle.

"Ready?" she asked.

Maddie nodded, because words wouldn't come.

They stepped onto the circle to join Lulu. As soon as they did, Maddie felt a jolt. On the one hand, she knew this was just a piece of wood, like any other. But, if she closed her eyes, she could also feel the energy and rhythm of all the people who'd sang on this spot before.

A burst of confidence surged through her. What was she afraid of? No one was watching, and she'd sung with her sisters hundreds of times before. Now, they would be singing to the rafters of the Opry. Why not?

"Let's practice our song," Mia said, and launched into their arrangement of "This Little Light of Mine." It was harder to keep the rhythm and pace without the guitars and drums backing them up, but their harmonies sounded strong. As they got going, Maddie lost herself in the song. They sang and sang, all the way to the final notes, and then, breathless, took a bow.

From the wings, someone started clapping. Maddie whipped around and saw that it wasn't just one someone. Mom, Dad, Miss Julia, Amanda, and even some of the band members were all beaming and applauding.

Lulu gave an elaborate curtsey. Mia reached out for Maddie's hand so they could bow together too. Maddie had to admit, it felt good having everyone cheering them on. No one seemed a bit upset that they were standing on the circle, either. Even so, she carefully edged off the wooden planks, just in case.

"So, are the girls going to sing on Friday night?" Richie, the drummer, asked. "Sounds to me like they're ready."

"We'll see." Mom's face glowed with happiness.

Maddie tried very hard not to look out at all those seats. Hopefully, if they did sing, the lights would be so bright that she could pretend Friday was just like tonight, with only this small circle of friends watching. Maybe she could pretend that anyway. Her heart thumped inside her chest, and she had to admit, it wasn't just from fear. If she was being honest with herself, she really had enjoyed standing on the circle and singing with her sisters.

Mom scooped the girls into a giant hug. "And now it's time to put my beautiful girls to bed. Ready to go home?"

"Ready," they all agreed.

TEN

L et's have a quick snuggle before lights out," Mom said.

All three girls piled into Mia's bed, making room for Mom. Maddie leaned her head against Mom's shoulder, and Lulu curled up right next to Maddie. Mia sat on Mom's other side. Mom wrapped her arms around all three girls and gave them a squeeze. "I was so proud of my beautiful girls tonight. Your singing was fantastic, but my favorite part was watching all three of you up there, having so much fun together."

"So you're going to let us sing on Friday?" Lulu grabbed Mom's hand and pressed it against her own heart. "We'll sing just as good, I promise!"

"Just as well," Mom corrected, tucking a piece of hair behind Lulu's ear. "It's not that I don't think you'll do a great job, Lulu. The thing is, performing is all about the heart."

"You mean singing with all our hearts?" Lulu said. "Because we are, we truly are."

"I know you are, sweetheart. The thing is, performers need to love Jesus more than they love being on stage."

"But we do love Jesus," Mia said.

Mom untangled herself so she could sit facing the girls, and looked them each in the eyes. "You know that feeling of being swept up into the music? And how it felt tonight when everyone was clapping for you?"

"Because we were awesome!" Lulu swept her hand above her head like she was spelling their names out in lights. "Glimmer Girls take the stage!"

Mom nodded, and Maddie could see she was trying hard to put her concern into words.

"You mean we might get too excited about the applause and not remember that we're singing about Jesus?" Maddie wondered if this might happen to her. More likely, she'd be wondering what everyone was thinking of her. Still, those thoughts could definitely get in the way of thinking about the meaning of the song.

"Exactly," Mom said. "And even when your song isn't a praise song—even then—performing isn't about being the center of attention. Whenever we use our gifts, we're giving our best for God. It's not about how much applause we might get."

Mia frowned and pulled a pillow into her lap. Maddie could see she was thinking hard. "How do you know if you're thinking in the right way? I mean, when I'm singing, I do think about the words, but I'm also thinking about the melody and the harmony and the beat. Is that wrong?"

"No, that's not wrong," Mom said. "Not at all."

"So what are we doing wrong?" Lulu asked.

Mom reached out to squeeze each of their shoulders. "You're not doing anything wrong. And I do think you girls should sing on Friday night. The reason Dad and I have talked about it for a while is because we love you and we want to help you. It's not easy to make sure your heart is right when you're onstage. In fact, it's a constant struggle."

"Even for you?" Maddie asked.

"Even for me," Mom admitted. "We want people to applaud us and tell us we're doing a great job. There's a constant need to point back to the giver of the gift, not to the gift itself. Whatever skills we're developing, we're learning to use the gift God has given to us."

"Wait a second." Lulu grabbed both of Mom's hands, her expression serious. "Did you just say you're going to let us sing?"

Mom smiled a quiet smile. "I did say that."

"Awwwesome!" Lulu whooped, jumping out of bed and bouncing around the room.

Mia sprang out of bed too, launching into a happy dance. "Yes, yes, yesssss!"

"And what about you, Maddie?" Mom laced her fingers through Maddie's. "What do you think about singing on Friday?"

Maddie watched her sisters celebrating and shrieking, and wondered why it didn't quite feel that way for her.

"What on earth is going on in here?" Dad asked, leaning on the doorframe.

"We're going to sing, we're going to sing, we're going to sing!" Lulu chanted.

Maddie couldn't help catching a little of their enthusiasm, especially when Mom looked her straight in the eyes and gave her a special smile all her own. "You're going to be fantastic, Maddie."

Nodding, Maddie felt her own smile growing. "We're going to sing at the Opry!"

"At the Opry!" Mia echoed.

"And then, when we finish our song, someone will come out on stage and invite us all to be members. And we'll be the youngest members of the Opry ever," Lulu said.

Mom and Dad burst out laughing.

"I don't know about that," Mom said. "But seriously now, girls, come over here. We have something important to talk to you about."

Mia and Lulu climbed back into the bed, and Dad joined them too.

Mom looked up at Dad, and he said, "When you take the stage, everyone's going to clap and scream for you because you're young and adorable."

"You know we're very proud of you," Mom continued. "You see how I show you off on social media all the time. You're smart, beautiful, and talented. But even when everyone is cheering for you after you've sung your hearts out, I want you to remember that whatever we do, we do it to reflect God's presence in our lives."

Dad nodded. "Especially in this benefit, we're performing for an important reason—to raise money to help others who need warm food and safe homes."

"I think I can do that," Lulu said. "But I just love performing. Right before I go out on stage, I get really nervous. But then when people start to clap, it makes me so happy, I feel like my heart will explode."

"That's what we're talking about," Mom said. "It's easy to get caught up in that feeling and forget who gave us our gifts in the first place."

"But I think I can do it," Lulu repeated. "I really, really think I can."

"I think so too." Mom pulled Lulu into her arms.

"Me too." Mia leaned into the hug, wrapping her arms around Lulu and Mom.

"Me three," Maddie said, joining them.

"All right, it's settled," Mom said. "We'll rehearse your song tomorrow with the full band."

"What's that I hear?" Dad tilted his head as though he was straining to hear something far down the hall. "Hummm, hummm, hummm . . . I think the Daddy Monster is on his way!"

Dad tickled the girls while they shrieked and giggled. Mom smothered them with kisses until they were all laughing so hard they could hardly breathe.

"Okay, time for bed, sweet girls," Mom said.

"Can we say our prayers all together?" Lulu asked.

"Sure," Mom said. "Would you like to pray, Lulu?"

"Yep!" Lulu closed her eyes, and everyone else did too. "God, thank you, thank you, thank you that we get to sing on Friday night. And after we sing, when everyone claps and cheers, help us to remember what Mommy said about our hearts. And also, help all the people who don't have houses or food. In Jesus' name . . ."

". . . Amen," they all said.

Mom shooed Lulu and Maddie toward the door. "Now off to bed with you!"

Maddie crossed the hallway. She climbed into her bed and pulled her covers up around her ears.

"Good night," she called so everyone could hear.

"Good night," Mom called back.

"Sleep tight." Dad switched off Maddie's light. "And don't let any bedbugs bite!"

Maddie closed her eyes, and the quiet settled around her. Whatever happened on Friday night would happen. They were singing for God, and to help others who needed help. If she thought about those things instead of thinking about everything that might go wrong, she'd be able to sing without her legs going all wobbly. The Opry. She and her sisters were going to sing at the Opry!

ELEVEN

And then, we stepped onto the circle, the real Grand Ole Opry circle!" Mia said to Annabeth and Emily out at recess the next day.

She demonstrated by stepping onto one of the thick, ropy roots of their oak tree. The girls' hair whipped around their faces. The wind had kept up since yesterday, and Maddie was pretty sure it would rain any minute.

"So, you're actually going to sing at the Opry on Friday?" Emily asked.

"I think so," Maddie said, her throat tightening at the thought.

"You don't have to look upset about it," Annabeth said. "We know you're excited—you don't have to pretend you're not."

"I . . ." Maddie had no idea how to explain the way it felt looking out at all those seats and imagining all those eyes looking at her.

"Annabeth," Mia said. "She's nervous. Can't you see that?"

"We're supposed to feel bad for you because you get to sing at the Opry?" Annabeth asked. "Don't you see how selfish that seems?"

"I didn't say . . ." Maddie felt like she was two steps behind everyone else in this conversation.

"She's not being selfish," Mia insisted.

"No, they're right." Maddie reached out for her sister's arm. "It's special to sing at the Opry. I should be excited. I am excited."

"It's okay for you to feel nervous, though," Mia said.

"Can we please talk about something other than the Opry?" Annabeth caught her hair and wrestled with the wind to get it under control.

"Like your dance?" Mia snapped.

And there it was, the dance again. Maddie cringed, knowing this wouldn't be good.

"What's your problem?" Annabeth asked. "All week, you've been picking a fight with us. Just because we made our own dance while you were away on tour. We're not going to sit around doing nothing while you're off doing fun things."

Mia bit her lip. Maddie could see she wished she hadn't mentioned the dance just as much as Maddie did.

"I don't think . . ." Emily said, causing everyone to stop talking. She hadn't said anything for such a long time that no one wanted to miss whatever it was she had to say. "I don't think we should be fighting like this. We're friends, and we're acting . . . well, not like friends. I don't know. Maybe we all need a little space. Maybe next week, after the Opry and everything, we can start over."

Maddie's mouth went dry. Space? Things were that bad?

When no one said anything, Emily seemed to feel the need to explain. "I just don't want to fight."

"Me neither," Maddie said.

"I think space is a good idea," Annabeth said.

Mia didn't say anything at all. Maddie could almost hear her sister's mind racing back and forth, searching for a way to patch things up. None of them wanted to be in a fight, but every topic was a possible explosion. The gap between the girls and their friends grew wider all the time—exactly the way Maddie feared it would after coming home from tour.

"I don't know what to say," Mia said.

Maddie had to agree. What was there to say?

"Umm . . . So, maybe we should go work on our dance, then," Emily said.

Annabeth took off for the other side of the playground, where they'd been practicing yesterday. Emily stood there for a moment, not saying anything. Maddie didn't say anything either. The only word she could think of was *space*. Finally, Emily smiled a sad smile and turned to follow Annabeth. Maddie sat, her back pressed against the tree, exactly where she had been yesterday. Space. Her friends needed space? Space was the exact thing that Maddie didn't want.

"I can't believe they're doing this," Mia said, flopping down next to Maddie. "It's totally unfair for them to be mad at us, just because we're singing at the Opry. They're the ones being selfish."

"I don't know," Maddie said.

"They never even apologized for making up a dance that purposely left us out. Then, when we showed them our dance, they didn't have anything nice to say. They weren't like this last year. What's wrong?"

"I don't know," Maddie repeated.

"And we're supposed to be feeling bad, while they're over there, doing their dance over and over again. They're the ones leaving us out. It's not fair!"

Maddie dropped her forehead into her hands.

"Maddie?" Mia asked. "Don't you agree?"

"I don't know," Maddie repeated, her temper starting to flare. "Did you have to bring up the dance again today, Mia? You knew they were already upset—"

"For unfair reasons," Mia said.

"I know it feels that way."

"It *is* that way, Maddie. You know it is. And now, they're 'taking space.'" Mia made air quotes. "Which means they won't even come to our Opry debut. They're our best friends, Maddie, so shouldn't they be there for us?"

Maddie thought about it, and finally said, "I only want them to be there if they really want to be."

At this, all the fire fizzled out of Mia. "Yeah. I guess you're right."

Maddie looked up, through the wind-whipped branches of the tree, at the darkening, gray sky. Clouds scudded by. A drip of water hit Maddie's nose, and then another struck her cheek.

"Time to go inside!" Mia said, helping Maddie to her feet.

They raced the rain, ducking under cover just as the skies opened up and poured down rain. Sheets of water soaked the blacktop and playground. Mr. Shelton blew his whistle, and everyone lined up to go inside. No one complained about recess being cut short. No one wanted to stay outside in the wet and cold. Maddie thought of those cardboard boxes out in the rain. Cardboard wouldn't keep a person dry in weather like this. No matter what happened with Annabeth and Emily, no matter how much she feared stepping out on that stage, she realized the chance to sing was a gift. By singing, she could do something to help people who truly needed help. *Keep people warm and dry,* she prayed silently as they filed inside. *And help me to be brave.*

TWELVE

Maddie and Mia peeked out of the wings, watching the band practice. The musicians had gone over one section of a song at least twenty times. Still, they kept going back to the beginning. Dad was in get-it-right mode. He did this with the girls too, insisting you shouldn't move on from an error until you got it right. "If you practice it wrong, you'll keep doing it wrong," he'd say. Most likely, he was right, but that didn't make Maddie much more patient about playing the same thing over and over. The band played the song through to the final notes . . . again.

Mom jogged over to talk with Mia and Maddie. "I'm sorry, girls, but it'll be a while until we can rehearse your song. Do you want to hang out with Lulu and Miss Julia in the dressing rooms?"

Mia shrugged. "I don't mind watching."

"Maybe we can do something to help with the auction?" Maddie suggested.

"Actually, that's a great idea," Mom said. "I set some cloths and instrument polish on the table in the studio. Would you like to give the instruments a final polish, so there are no leftover fingerprints on them? You can also fluff the tissue paper in the baskets. We finished arranging the items, but didn't pretty them up yet."

"That would be fun!" Mia said.

"We'll be careful," Maddie assured Mom.

Mom kissed her hands and pressed the kisses against the girls' cheeks. "I'll come get you when it's time for your song. I promise we'll try our hardest to rehearse it tonight, girls. You've been so patient." Mom started back across the stage, but stopped. "Oh, and if you need anything, don't forget Miss Julia is in the dressing rooms. Just around the corner from the studio. You'll be okay?"

"We'll be great!" Mia said.

"Yep, great!" Maddie echoed.

She and Mia walked through the wings, wound through the back hallways, and found their way to the studio.

"Which thing would you buy, if you could buy anything?" Mia asked Maddie.

"Probably the painting that used to be in the Women in Country Music dressing room," Maddie said. "I like it because it's from the Opry, but it's also a really interesting painting. I like all the texture in the landscape. It reminds me of the London painting, remember?"

"You called the London painting 'Sun-Splattered Afternoon' because of all the texture," Mia said. "Yeah, I can see why you'd like that one."

The room was dark, so Mia fiddled with the lightboard switches. "Where do you turn on the lights, anyway?"

"Are you sure you should be touching that?" Maddie asked.

Mom was always telling them not to touch light- or soundboards. Technicians set them specific ways and didn't appreciate people moving the dials around.

"We can't just trip around in the dark back here," Mia said.

"I guess that's true," Maddie said.

"There!" Mia said, as the lights blazed to life.

Stage lights hung on pipes that stretched the length of the studio. Their colors mixed to throw a warm glow over the tables and auction items.

"How do people bid on the items?" she asked Mia.

"That's what the clipboards are for. Once the items are in the lobby, people will write their names and their bids—"

"What?" Maddie asked, as Mia's voice trailed off. Mia had such an odd look on her face.

"The guitar," Mia said. "Where is it?"

"Ms. Carpenter's guitar?" Maddie asked. "It's right next to the middle table on the—Wait."

"Yeah." Mia motioned to the empty stand. "Shouldn't it be right there?"

"We should go tell someone," Maddie said.

"But we can't interrupt the rehearsal," Mia said.

"So, let's find Miss Julia then," Maddie said.

"Someone. Mia, we have to do something right now."

"Yeah, okay," Mia said. "Come on."

Maddie took off running after Mia, silently arguing with herself. No one would have actually taken the guitar. It must be misplaced or something. All she could think of was that empty stand with no guitar in it.

"Where are you girls off to in such a hurry?" Charles asked from behind the security desk as they blasted past.

Maddie made the effort to slow down and answer. "Did you see where Miss Julia went?"

"She and your sister are back in the Cousin Minnie room," he said. "Is everything okay?"

"I think . . ." Maddie started to say, but Mia was already off running again. "We'll explain in a minute!"

"Miss Julia, Miss Julia!" Mia called as they careened down the hallway and around the corner.

"Whoa, whoa, whoa!" Miss Julia caught Mia before she barreled her over. Maddie was only steps behind, but breathing hard.

Miss Julia held Mia at arm's length so she could look into her eyes. "What is it?"

"The guitar is missing!" Mia said.

Only then did Maddie realize Lulu was wearing boots that came up to her hips. "Where did you get those?"

"Focus, Maddie!" Mia said.

"They're for my costume!" Lulu said, swinging her arms wide to show off the rest of her ensemble.

"No—we're trying on some Opry costumes," Miss Julia corrected. "Your mom will want to dress you up in something that fits you properly. We're just having fun."

"Isn't this hat bea-u-tiful?" Lulu asked.

"Didn't anyone hear me?" Mia asked. "The guitar is missing!"

"It is." Maddie gasped, and as she said this to Miss Julia, the weight of the situation settled in. Ms. Carpenter had donated a valuable guitar, and now it was gone. Completely. All the money the guitar would have raised was lost too. What would Mom say? For that matter, what would Ms. Carpenter say?

"Which guitar?" Miss Julia asked. "Slow down, Mia, and explain."

"Earl Eldridge Jr.'s guitar," Mia said, only slowing her words the slightest bit. "It was on the guitar stand at that middle table, and now it's not there."

Miss Julia shook her head. "I'm sure it's there some-where, girls. Guitars don't sprout legs and walk away."

"It's worth a lot of money," Maddie said.

"No one at the Opry would walk off with a guitar," Miss Julia said. "And there's a security desk with staff watching the building all the time."

"But you don't have to pass through security to go to the studio," Mia insisted. "You can go straight across from the loading dock without coming backstage. Anyone could have come in through the doors and taken it."

"Before we panic, let's go take a look," Miss Julia said. "I'm sure you're mistaken."

"I can't walk in these," Lulu complained, tripping over her boots as she started down the hallway.

"Right," Miss Julia said. "Take them off and put them back in the dressing room. But then, put on your shoes. I don't want you walking around backstage without shoes on."

So, they had to wait while Lulu pulled off her boots, and then wait again until she found her shoes. Then, they had to wait some more as she tied them up, insisting she didn't want any help. Then, finally, finally, they were off again.

THIRTEEN

When they reached the studio, Miss Julia stopped and stared at the empty stand. "The guitar was right there."

"And now it's gone!" Mia repeated, her voice rising in frustration. Not being believed was one of Mia's least-favorite situations, and Maddie knew her sister was about to lose it.

Miss Julia crossed the room, as though taking a closer look at the stand would help. No guitar. She did a slow walk of the room, looking behind and under the tables.

"It's not here." Mia paced, back and forth, back and forth. Maddie didn't blame her. She couldn't stand still either.

"That doesn't mean that someone took it—" Miss Julia began, but before she could finish her thought, Lulu was already running out of the room.

"Where's she going?" Mia asked.

"Lulu, wait!" called Miss Julia.

Maddie figured Lulu was headed straight for the stage. Mom wouldn't be happy to have rehearsal interrupted, but maybe Lulu was right. Mom and Dad should know about the guitar right away. Who knew how long it had been missing? Maybe if they looked right away, they could still find the thief. If, in fact, there was a thief.

Miss Julia hurried after Lulu, with Mia close behind. Maddie brought up the rear, wondering whether they should stop and tell Charles. Everyone else blasted past his desk, so she kept going too, not wanting to be left behind.

"The guitar is missing, the guitar is missing!" Lulu called as she ran onto the stage. "Help!"

The music broke off abruptly as Mia, Maddie, and Miss Julia joined Lulu. Eight pairs of eyes turned to stare.

"What . . . Miss Julia, what's going on here?" Dad asked.

"Didn't you hear what I said?" Lulu asked, a perfect echo of Mia from just minutes ago. "The guitar is missing!"

"Earl Eldridge Jr.'s guitar," Mia clarified.

Maddie nodded in agreement.

Mom blinked at the girls as though she wasn't quite processing what they were saying. "I'm sure you must be mistaken."

"That's what I told them," Miss Julia said. "What I was about to say, Lulu, before you ran off, was that someone must have taken the guitar off the stand for a purpose. Maybe someone is tuning it, or adjusting the bridge or something. I'm sure the guitar hasn't been stolen."

Maddie knew Miss Julia meant to be reassuring, but as soon as she said the word *stolen*, no one else said anything for almost a minute. The possibility of the guitar actually being gone—gone for good—settled across the stage.

"No . . ." Mom finally broke the silence. "No one would have taken the guitar off the stand. We didn't want to do any repairs or tuning. Part of the guitar's charm is that it remains unchanged from when Earl Eldridge Jr. himself used it."

"Did anyone move the guitar?" Dad asked the rest of the band members.

Silently, all heads shook no. The stage was nearly as quiet as it had been yesterday when Mia, Maddie, and Lulu had been alone in the wings.

"I looked all around the studio, under and behind tables, but didn't see anything," Miss Julia said.

"I suppose we should speak with security, then." Mom placed her microphone in the stand. "Maybe Charles or one of the others saw something. Or maybe someone moved the guitar without mentioning it to us."

"And if they didn't, we can look in all the rooms," Lulu said. "A Grand Ole Opry treasure hunt!"

"This isn't a game," Mia told Lulu.

"I know it's not a game," Lulu said, hands on hips. "But how are we going to find the guitar if we don't look for it?"

"Come on," Maddie said. "They're leaving without us."

Everyone—Mom, Dad, Miss Julia, the band, and the girls—filed back through the wings, around the corner, and crammed into the small entryway by the security desk.

"What's happening? The girls ran by a few minutes ago, but no one told me . . ." Charles must have seen the grim look on Mom's face, because he said with concern, "What is it?"

"One of the auction items—Earl Eldridge Jr.'s guitar—is missing," Mom said. "We're hoping maybe one of your staff moved it for some reason."

"Oh, no, Gloria," he said. "We'd never have moved any of your items without asking you first."

"Yes, I thought that was likely the case," Mom said.

"So, it *is* stolen?" Lulu asked, her voice rising.

"We don't know that," Dad said, wrapping his arms around all three girls and pulling them close.

Charles stood and consulted his monitors. "When was the last time you saw the guitar?"

"I wish it had been tonight," Mom said. "I took some cloths and polish back there and set them on a table on our way in. I didn't think to turn on the lights or check the auction items. So, the last time I'm sure the guitar was there is last night."

"That's a long stretch of time," Charles said. "I can start to review security footage for you, but reviewing that much video will take at least until tomorrow. I don't have a camera facing the studio, but we do have one by the stage door, and a few others scattered through the building. We may be able to find someone who looks like he or she isn't supposed to be here. That would be a start, anyway."

"Thank you," Mom said.

"Can we look around?" Lulu asked. "Just in case?"

"Yes, I think we should look around." Mom checked her watch. "But it's getting late. We'll need to leave in about twenty minutes. Girls, I don't think we'll have time to rehearse your song now."

"I don't feel like singing right now anyway," Mia said.

Maddie didn't either. Of all the items—even the painting that she loved—having the guitar go missing was the worst. Not just because it would probably bring the highest bids in the auction. E. E. Jr. had loved his guitar, and Ms. Carpenter had treasured it. Most valuable things could be replaced, but this guitar was a loved and treasured item, one of a kind. What would they tell Ms. Carpenter?

"I'll check the wings," Mia said. "I saw a big guitar rack. Maybe the guitar was accidentally mixed in with the others."

"That's a good idea," Maddie agreed.

"I want to come too!" Lulu said.

Everyone split up. The girls and Miss Julia went to the wings to check the guitar rack. Mom, Dad, and the band handled the studio, the area around it, and the dressing rooms.

"We'll find the guitar, Mom, I'm sure we will," Lulu called.

Maddie hoped Lulu was right, but she wasn't so sure.

FOURTEEN

ack through the darkened wings one more time,
Lulu made a beeline for the guitar racks. Light
from the stage made enough of a glow that they could
see, but only dimly. Miss Julia took out her phone and
used its flashlight function to look more closely. Maddie
walked a full circle around the racks, hoping she'd see
a worn-out-looking guitar. Unfortunately, none of the
guitars looked anything like Earl Eldridge Jr.'s guitar.

"We should pick them each up." Lulu lifted one
slightly and tried to check the bottom.

"Careful, Lulu!" Mia said.

"Mia's right, Lulu," Miss Julia said. "I'm not sure we
should pick them up."

"But how are we supposed to look for a chip when
they're all smoothed together in the rack like this?"
Lulu asked, bending down, trying to see.

"The rest of the guitar would look worn-out too,"
Mia said. "Remember how old his guitar looked, Lulu?"

"But if someone polished it, it might be shiny and
new-looking like these."

"Maybe . . ." Mia said.

"Definitely," Lulu said.

"How about I lift them and you look underneath,"
Miss Julia suggested, handing Lulu her phone, so Lulu

89

could shine the light on each guitar and look more closely.

Maddie didn't have much hope that they'd find the guitar this way, but she didn't have any other ideas to suggest. This summer, when they'd seen a thief steal a painting off the wall at London's National Gallery of Art, it hadn't been like this. They hadn't had to poke around in the dark with no idea who had taken the painting. Maybe tomorrow, once Charles had reviewed the tapes, it would be easier to do something. Right now, the whole thing felt a little hopeless.

"You okay, Maddie?" Mia asked.

"It hasn't been a very good day," Maddie said.

"Yeah, you're right," Mia said.

"I was thinking about what you said, about whether I wanted Annabeth and Emily to come to the concert," Maddie said. "I'm still nervous about singing, especially now that we didn't practice tonight. But I do wish they'd come. I mean, I really want them to want to come."

"Me too."

They watched Lulu and Miss Julia move from guitar to guitar, Miss Julia lifting, and Lulu checking.

"Why do you think they're so mad at us?" Mia asked Maddie. "I don't understand."

Maddie had noticed a few things, like the way Annabeth tensed up every time Mia talked about their competing dances. It seemed, though, that the problem was bigger than the dances. Especially with the way

Annabeth kept mentioning their tour and everything they got to do because they were Glimmer girls.

"I don't think we're any different this year than we were last year," she said. "Are we?"

"I don't know," Mia said.

"Annabeth said we are being selfish," Maddie said. "And if we are, of course that would make them upset. But I don't understand what we're being selfish about."

"I think they're just a little jealous," Mia said.

Maddie didn't have a good answer for this. Maybe their friends did feel a little jealous, but wasn't that how friends felt every once in a while? She felt that way sometimes, anyway. And even though the idea of singing at the Opry scared her, she'd definitely feel left out if Mia and Lulu were going to perform without her. Feeling left out was what had started all this in the first place—that closed-out feeling she'd had watching her friends dance. And now, she and Mia had the concert on Friday with no room in it for Annabeth and Emily. Since they couldn't include their friends in the performance, maybe there was a way to help them feel less closed out.

"Maybe there's something we can do to include them," she told Mia.

"In the concert?" Mia frowned. "How would we do that?"

"Maybe not in the concert, but in the benefit . . . I don't know," Maddie said. "I'll think about it."

"It's not here." Lulu checked the bottom of the last guitar and sighed.

"Let's go see what the others have found," Miss Julia said.

Unfortunately, no one had better news. They'd scoured the dressing rooms and backstage areas, and the guitar was nowhere to be found. Dad checked in at the security desk, and Charles hadn't spotted anything on the video footage, either.

"We'll have to postpone the search until tomorrow," Mom said. "Maybe by then, Charles will have found something."

"Will he sit there all night reviewing the videos from the security cameras?" Maddie asked. She wanted to find the thief, but she didn't want Charles to have to work all through the night.

"I'm sure he'll go home when his shift ends," Dad said. "And someone else can pick up the search tomorrow morning."

"Maybe whoever took the guitar will decide they don't want it after all," Maddie said.

"If he went to all the trouble to steal it, why would he give it back?" Mia asked.

"You never know," Dad said. "Especially since this is a charity benefit. If we spread the word about the missing guitar and why it's important to the cause, maybe the thief will have a change of heart."

"Speaking of the cause, let's head on out to the car, girls," Mom said. "Tomorrow, you need all your energy. We're going to Third Street to help serve lunch."

"We're going to the shelter tomorrow?" Mia asked.

"We're not going to school?" Maddie didn't want to miss any more time with Annabeth and Emily, even if they were 'taking space.' Maybe by tomorrow, everything would have blown over.

"I thought it would be nice for you girls to see what our concert and auction is all about," Mom said. "You can go to school in the morning, and Miss Julia will pick you up a little before lunch."

"And then we can warm people's bellies, like Earl Eldridge Jr. did," Lulu said.

Dad grinned. "What's that?"

"One of the Opry staff told us some stories about him—about when he used to serve food at a soup kitchen. E. E. Jr. said he didn't only want to warm people's bellies, but their hearts too," Maddie explained.

"If anyone can warm hearts," Dad said, wrapping them into a hug, "I'm sure my girls can. Now, off to the car with you, and I'll see you at home to tuck you into bed."

"See you soon," the girls said.

FIFTEEN

After they'd all buckled in, Mom sat in the car with the ignition off for a moment.

"I suppose I should call Jennifer," she said to Miss Julia.

"Everything will work out," Miss Julia said. "Maybe we can't see how right now, but God can work a miracle here."

"Wouldn't it be amazing if God could find the guitar wherever it is, and move it back to the studio where it's supposed to be?" Mia said.

"You mean like with superpowers?" Maddie said.

"I guess that's kind of what I mean," Mia said. "But I know God doesn't work that way. Maybe he'd use angels."

"God can do those kinds of things," Mom said. "In the Bible, he talks about faith being able to move mountains. You know, Mia, that's an important reminder. Before we do anything else, we should definitely pray."

"Can I do it?" Lulu asked.

"Of course," Mom said.

They all bowed their heads. Maddie tried to quiet the worries bouncing around in her mind, but it was hard, even with her eyes closed.

"God, somehow Earl Eldridge's guitar got lost," Lulu said. "We don't know what happened, but we looked everywhere in the Opry, and we can't find it anywhere. You see everything, so I'm sure you know where it is. Please show us where to look, or help us find it. Pretty, pretty please?"

"Amen," Mom said. "Thank you, Lulu. You're right, God does see everything, and he knows where the guitar is. We'll trust that he'll help us figure this out in his timing."

"Sometimes it feels like God's timing takes such a long time," Mia said.

Mom laughed, and with her laughter, some of the heaviness in Maddie's chest lifted. If Mom could laugh even while the guitar was still missing, somehow, in some way, things would work out.

Mom turned the car on and backed up, dialing Ms. Carpenter on the speaker phone.

"Hi, Jennifer?" Mom said.

"Oh, hi there, Gloria," Ms. Carpenter said. "How is all the benefit prep?"

Mom took a deep breath, and Maddie took one right along with her. What would Ms. Carpenter say when she heard the news?

"That's actually why I'm calling," Mom said. "Unfortunately, I have bad news. I'm so sorry, but tonight while we were practicing, someone stole your grandfather's guitar. Or at least, that's how it appears.

The guitar may have been misplaced or moved, but we don't believe anyone in the Opry would have touched it. We searched the premises and haven't found it anywhere yet. In retrospect, I suppose there were many things we could have done to prevent something like this happening. We could have put locks on the studio doors, added more security monitoring, or even posted someone in the room with the items at all times. It just never occurred to us to think that anyone would steal items set aside for the auction. The building is pretty secure, and we didn't think . . . Oh, Jennifer, I'm so sorry."

Ms. Carpenter's voice was dull and missing all its usual brightness when she answered. "I'm sorry too, Gloria. What a terrible loss this is for everyone."

"We'll keep looking for the guitar, of course," Mom said.

"Of course," Ms. Carpenter echoed, but her voice didn't have much hope in it.

"I keep hoping the person who stole the guitar— whoever they are—will have a change of heart," Mom said.

"It's possible," Ms. Carpenter said.

"I know it's a long shot," Mom said. "We'll keep you informed as we continue to look."

"I appreciate that, Gloria," Ms. Carpenter said. "I should let you go. Sounds like you're driving home. Are the girls in the car with you?"

"We're here," Mia said.

"I'm so sorry, Ms. Carpenter," Maddie said, pushing the words out past the lump in her throat.

"I know you are, girls," Ms. Carpenter said. "I don't want you worrying. Okay? The benefit will be a success, even if the guitar isn't recovered. I know this situation will work out one way or another, even though it's hard to see how that will happen right now."

"Thanks, Jennifer," Mom said. "We'll see you tomorrow."

"See you tomorrow," she said.

Mom hung up, and no one spoke for a few minutes.

Finally, Mia broke the silence. "It's horrible, someone taking the guitar like that. Especially after Ms. Carpenter saved it for so long, waiting for just the right cause to donate it to."

"I don't want the guitar to have been stolen," Maddie said. "Do you really think that's what happened, Mom?"

"I'm not sure what else to think," Mom said. "It would be wonderful if the guitar is simply misplaced, but the likelihood of it being moved accidentally is pretty small."

"Maybe, like Mommy said, whoever took it will put it back," Lulu said.

"It's possible," Miss Julia said.

Maddie looked out the dark window at wet trees rushing by. Raindrops rolled down her window, reminding her of tears. Sometimes, when it rained, it made her wonder if God ever cried. Did the things people sometimes did—the wrong things—make him sad? It was a strange thought—God who was powerful enough to speak the entire universe into existence, with tears rolling down his face. Or maybe God didn't even have a face—she wasn't entirely sure. In the Old Testament, God appeared to the people as a pillar of fire in the nighttime and as a cloud in the day. But Jesus became a man and walked around with a living and breathing body. He'd eaten and slept. He'd even cried, actually. So, maybe sometimes God did cry.

Maddie spotted one star, and then another, between gaps in the clouds. She pressed her eyes closed and silently prayed, *God, please bring the guitar back. Help untangle everything that's knotted up with the benefit and with Annabeth and Emily, and with me too. Help us know what to do next.*

SIXTEEN

Waking up the next morning for school wasn't easy. Mom rubbed her shoulder, drawing Maddie out of her dreams. "I put out some clothes for you. And breakfast is ready downstairs. I let you girls sleep as long as I could, but now we need to hurry so you can make it to school on time."

Maddie blinked, and the room slowly came into focus. Her dream thoughts gave way to real-world thoughts. Pieces clicked into place. School—today might be their last chance to fix things with Annabeth and Emily before the concert. Everything that happened last night came to mind too. The guitar—and the conversation with Ms. Carpenter. Ms. Carpenter, who wouldn't be her usual cheerful self today at school. Even though Maddie knew the missing guitar wasn't her fault, she felt awful anyway.

The leggings, skirt, and shirt Mom had put out were perfect for today—soft, cozy, and easy to wear. Maddie finished dressing first and went to Mia's room.

"I dreamt last night that we found the guitar," Mia said, pulling on the skirt Mom had left out for her.

"Where?" Maddie asked.

"Well, it wouldn't happen like this in real life," Mia said. "In my dream, it was kind of like a treasure hunt, with clues left all over the Opry. We figured out each riddle, which led us to the next clue, and then Lulu finally found the guitar up in the light booth."

"I wish it could be like that, just a game," Maddie said.

"We're good at solving mysteries, though," Mia said. "Maybe we can figure this one out too."

Mom must have just finished waking Lulu up, because she passed by the door just then.

"Girls, are you dressed? Let's go eat."

Maddie had one more sock to pull on, which she did, and then hurried downstairs. As she passed through the kitchen, Dad stopped fiddling with the coffee maker and came over to plant a kiss on the top of her head.

"Morning, sweetheart," he said.

"Morning, Dad."

At the table, Mia was mid-conversation with Mom.

"We're not looking for mysteries," Mia insisted. "They just keep finding us."

"I was so proud of both of you this summer," Mom said. "You asked great questions and paid close attention. By doing that, you figured out what was going wrong at the water park, and also found the art thief in London. But, chasing after thieves can be dangerous."

"Extremely dangerous," Dad said, bringing a mug of coffee to Mom. "Think of how dangerous it was for Maddie to walk around London by herself chasing after her art thief. You've both promised never to do anything like that again."

"But in San Diego, we didn't break any rules," Mia said. "We just kept our eyes open."

"And you ended up spending your whole vacation looking for clues," Mom said.

"And riding water rides and seeing the dolphins," Mia said.

"And eating Belgian waffles!" Lulu added, bouncing into the room.

"Right now, it's time for you three to eat breakfast," Mom said. "I want you at school on time this morning, since we're pulling you out early."

Maddie spread raspberry jam on her toast and took a bite.

"All I'm saying is that sometimes we see things other people don't see," Mia said, after dutifully taking a bite of her toast too.

"That's true," Mom said. "But, we have your Opry debut on Friday night. That's a big deal, and to perform well, all three of you will need to focus. We don't need another wild goose chase."

"But we don't go on wild goose chases, Mom," Mia said. "We find thieves. Honestly, we've done it twice."

Mom smiled at this. To Maddie, it looked like she was trying hard not to, but couldn't stop herself.

"You're right about that," Mom said. "Let's take it one step at a time. School first, and then we'll head over to the shelter to serve lunch. Then, off to the Opry for rehearsal. Today, we're going to focus on your song first.

And while we're rehearsing, I don't want you distracted by anything—especially not by mysteries. Okay?"

"Do you think Charles or any of the other security guards found anything on the tapes?" Maddie asked.

Mom raised a warning eyebrow. "No worries about the guitar right now, okay? Trust Dad and me to keep working on it. We want to find the guitar just as much as you do. I promise."

"But if we see something, we should tell you, right?" Mia said.

When Mom looked over at Dad, the corners of her lips tilted up in a small smile. "Yes, of course, girls. If you see something, let us know."

"Glimmer girls to the rescue!" shouted Lulu, but then quickly added, "After we do all that other stuff Mommy wants us to do."

Maddie was almost finished with her toast when a new question struck her. "What will the shelter be like?"

She thought of the man they'd seen a few days ago, the one who had shouted at them. Would people at Third Street shout or ask questions she didn't have answers to? "Are we supposed to talk to the people?"

"We're supposed to tell them jokes, like Earl Eldridge Jr. did, right, Mommy?" Lulu asked.

Mom burst out laughing, and then came around the table, hugging each of them. "I love you all so much. When we're at the shelter, I want you to be your sparkly, kind selves. After all, Glimmer girls sparkle and shine . . ."

"But most of all, they are kind!" the girls said.

Miss Julia arrived right on cue, peeking her head in the front door. "Ready to load up?"

"Don't forget your backpacks!" Mom called as they all scurried to pull on their coats and shoes.

SEVENTEEN

Mom picked the girls up at the beginning of morning recess, which meant Maddie didn't have a chance to talk to Annabeth and Emily. It didn't matter much. Even if she'd had the chance, after thinking all morning, she hadn't come up with anything to say. Like Mia said, they couldn't include their friends in the performance. Without doing that, was there any way to fix Annabeth and Emily's hurt feelings? Hurt feelings were difficult. You couldn't fix them with a Band-aid or cough syrup.

"What are we supposed to do at the shelter?" Mia asked. "Are we cooking?"

"No, we'll be serving food," Mom said. "Denise, the shelter's director, is going to meet us today and explain what we'll each be doing."

"What if someone shouts at us?" Maddie asked.

"I'm sure no one will shout," Mom said. "But we'll all be together behind the tables, so if you need me, I'll be right there to help you."

The shelter was a brick building right in the middle of downtown. After they circled the block a few times, they ended up parking in a garage. When they came around the corner from Third Street onto Broadway, Maddie saw a line of people waiting to go inside. There

were people of all ages, which surprised Maddie.
She even saw a few kids. Their clothing was frayed
around the edges or even had holes. Most of them were
wearing coats, but they still looked cold. Maddie was
grateful that at least it wasn't raining anymore.

"Are they all shelter people?" Lulu asked.

Mom smoothed down a wild hair on Lulu's head.
"They are using the shelter's services, sweetie, but I
wouldn't call them shelter people."

Lulu stopped and tilted her head up at Mom, con-
fused. "Why not?"

"It's easy for people to forget how special they are
to God, especially when they start labeling themselves.
When a person needs help, that doesn't mean they are
forever-after a needy person. It's important to remember
that our life situations don't change who we are."

"You mean all those people are homeless?" Mia asked.
"None of them have places to sleep, even the kids?"

Maddie thought of those sheets of rain. Some of the
children in the line were younger than Lulu. No one
should sleep outside on the soggy ground, but the idea
of a tiny child huddled up in the rain, trying to sleep,
was terrible.

"If they're here for a meal, they definitely need some
help, one way or the other." Mom pointed to a side door.
"Others, who are already inside, stay here at the shelter,
at least for now, until they're able to afford their own
place to live."

"Then why doesn't everyone stay here?" Maddie asked. "So no one has to sleep outside?"

"There are only so many beds," Mom said. "But that's one of the things we're trying to do with our benefit. Some of the money will go to buying more food, so people can continue to have warm meals. And some will go toward creating space for more temporary housing."

"Will we raise enough so they'll all have somewhere to sleep?" Lulu eyed the line of people.

"I wish we could, sweetheart," Mom said. "Homelessness is a big problem. Not just because we need more space, but also because many people aren't ready to ask for help."

Maddie's stomach growled. She'd only had time for one piece of toast that morning, and since they hadn't stayed for recess, she'd missed her morning snack. But she was only a little bit hungry—missed-snack hungry. What would it feel like to wake up to a completely empty stomach, and then to have to choose whether to ask someone for food or go hungry? Every single person in that line had to stand on the street for everyone to see.

"How do they decide who gets to stay at the shelter, then?" Mia asked. "If they can't help everyone?"

"They keep a waiting list," Mom said. "And while people are at the shelter, they are given their own roles so they can contribute. One of the first steps is for people to understand they each have gifts to give, no matter what might have gone wrong for them. The staff also helps shelter residents work toward finding jobs. They offer classes, training, and counseling. Once a family is able to move to their own apartment, space opens up for someone new." Mom checked her watch. "It's time for us to go inside. These are all such great questions, girls. I'm sure you'll have more after lunch, and on the way to the Opry, we can talk about this more. Okay?"

The girls nodded. The minute Mom opened the door, they were swept inside by a woman who seemed to fill the whole room.

"Welcome, ladies," she said, shaking each of their hands.

Her hands were gentle and warm. She wore a flour-streaked apron that had a slight scent of vanilla and cinnamon. She'd braided and wrapped her salt-and-pepper hair around her head.

"Excuse my appearance. Rachelle and I just finished baking a batch of snickerdoodles for today's crowd—her family recipe, and delicious, I must say," she said. "Gloria, we're so grateful for all that you and your team are doing for Third Street. And girls, I hear that you're going to sing at the benefit too? What a special gift you're giving to support our community."

"It's our Opry debut!" Lulu said.

"Denise," Mom said. "I don't know if you heard that our most valuable donation—Earl Eldridge Jr.'s guitar—has gone missing. We're so disappointed."

Denise shook her head and took Mom's hand again. "If there's one thing I learned during my time as a resident of Third Street, and over and over again after working here for all these years, it's that God works in mysterious ways. Sometimes it's hard to see why one thing or another happens, and then down the road, *wham!* You understand. And other times, well . . . you keep on waiting. But for now, let's not be disappointed. Let's not worry, but in all things, give thanks."

"Amen," Mom said.

"You were a . . ." Maddie broke off her question as she realized she had no polite way to ask whether Denise meant she had once been homeless. It was hard to imagine this full-of-life, joyful woman huddling under a cardboard box.

"After I went back to school and made some big changes in my life," Denise said, "I decided to come back to Third Street. During my stay here, I learned that I did have something important to give, and I wanted to help others discover that truth too. People think the hardest part of being poor is not having things that other people have. Actually, the worst thing is forgetting that you have something worthy to offer. If you think you're worthless, it's easy to give up."

Maddie thought about this for a moment, realizing that up to this point, she'd only been thinking about raising money to help the people at Third Street. But, maybe money wasn't the most important thing they needed. Butterflies filled her stomach at the thought of going out and serving food. What if she said or did the wrong things?

Mia reached over and squeezed her hand, and Maddie realized her sister must be thinking similar thoughts.

"Now, let's head on into the kitchen so we can set you up before the crowd descends," Denise said, and then grinned at the girls. "How do you ladies feel about hairnets?"

"Hair whats?" Lulu asked.

Denise burst out laughing. "Leave your coats here in this closet, and then this way, ladies! Come on through here."

Dad had said they could warm people's hearts, but how? Well, probably by smiling and listening and treating them with respect. And maybe Lulu could make them laugh a little too.

EIGHTEEN

We absolutely have to wear these things?" Mia asked for the third time, tugging at her hairnet's elastic band.

Maddie fiddled with her elastic too, trying to arrange it so it didn't feel so tight around her forehead. Lulu pulled her hairnet down over her chin.

"Lulu." Mom looked so funny with her hair all stuffed up in the net.

Maddie was used to seeing her sisters looking silly. Especially Lulu, with the wild outfits she sometimes chose, but Mom always looked like . . . Mom. Whether she was in her high heels or wide-brimmed floppy hats or both, Mom always had that Gloria Glimmer style. Hairnets were, well, not so Gloria Glimmer.

Lulu sighed and returned the net to its proper place. Denise handed out aprons too. The aprons were all adult-sized, so they had to wrap the apron strings round and round to make them work. Maddie and Mia's aprons touched the floor. Lulu's dragged so much that Denise suggested they fold it in half and try again.

"Let's all wash our hands now," Denise said. "And after that, no touching your hair or faces. If you do, you'll need to come back here and wash up again."

They took turns squeezing soap onto their palms, and washed between their fingers and under their fingernails. Then, they pulled on plastic gloves.

Denise gave them stations right next to each other at the end of the line. Mom had tongs and a giant bowl of veggie-filled salad. Maddie was in charge of ladling creamy tomato soup into bowls. Mia had crunchy rolls to hand out, and Lulu got to add the final snickerdoodle cookie treat. Denise and Tony, a resident of Third Street, were in charge of the lasagna and pasta options.

"When you run out," Denise said, "call on back to Zanne, and she'll bring you another batch. Any questions before Henry opens the door?"

"I think we're set," Mom said, and then gave the girls a reassuring smile. "You'll do great."

As soon as Henry opened the door, Maddie's worries evaporated. She didn't have time to think about anything except for putting soup in bowls.

"Thank you," a woman said, causing Maddie to stop and look up. The deep lines around the woman's eyes didn't take away from the spark of something . . . what? Happiness? Maddie smiled at the woman, remembering that while handing out soup was her task, what she truly wanted to do was to warm hearts.

Maddie looked past the woman to the room beyond. The tables were starting to fill up. Rather than being heavy with sadness and gloom—the way Maddie realized she'd been expecting it to be—the room was warm,

colorful, and filled with laughter and lively conversation. In fact, as she watched, the warmth spread into her
too, making her eyes fill with happy tears. Honestly, it
felt like she was the one who was being given the gift.

"Thank *you*," she echoed back, truly grateful that
this woman had interrupted her busyness to help her
see what was all around her.

The woman winked at Maddie and then raised a
mischievous eyebrow at Lulu. "Snickerdoodles are my
favorite."

"Give her an extra one," Maddie whispered to her
sister, who slipped an extra cookie onto the woman's tray.

The woman beamed at the girls. "Many thanks,
girls. Many thanks."

After that, Maddie made an effort to look each
person in the eyes as they passed in the line. Rather
than being a crowd of sad people, she started to see
that each person was unique, each had a story. There
were people of all ages. Some looked worn down and
exhausted, but others bubbled along through the line,
joyful and full of thanks.

"People aren't the way I thought they'd be," Mia
said quietly to Maddie. "I thought they'd be . . ."

"Sad?" Maddie said.

"Yeah, I guess," Mia said. "And different."

Maddie turned her attention back to the line, ready
to pour soup into the next bowl. The girl standing
across from her wore her pretty black hair straight.

This girl had to be about Maddie's age. Maddie's hand hovered over the girl's plate. She'd smiled at people, but hadn't said anything to anyone. Now, it seemed she should say . . . something.

"I'm Maddie," she said, setting a bowl on the girl's plate.

The girl smiled, and when she did a deep dimple creased her left cheek. "I'm Ruby."

"Want a snickerdoodle, Ruby?" Lulu asked.

"Are you kidding?" Ruby said. "Yeah, for sure. Rachelle's snickerdoodles are the best around."

"So you come here a lot?" Maddie asked.

Mia elbowed her, and Maddie realized her question had sounded strange, as though this were a restaurant, not a homeless shelter.

"I mean . . ."

"We're staying here at Third Street right now." Ruby gestured to a woman and little boy a few people back in line. The woman was deep in conversation, so she hadn't seemed to notice the hold up in the line. "My mom, my little brother, and me. My dad refuses to stay with us, but he still comes every day to see us outside after lunch. We'll get to see him soon."

"Ruby," her mom said. "We should keep moving along."

"Right." Ruby gave the girls another dimpled smile. "Guess I have to go. I heard you might sing today, though. Is that true?"

"I don't . . ." Maddie looked at Mia, who shrugged.

"Well, I love music," Ruby said, grinning. "So I hope you do!"

Lulu put a second snickerdoodle on Ruby's plate too, and then the line started moving again.

"Mom, are we singing?" Maddie asked.

"I don't know," Mom said. "I think they do sing a bit after everyone eats. Worship songs. We'll see."

NINETEEN

Zanne kept bringing food, and they kept serving until everyone in the line had their fill. Some even came back for seconds.

"Some of the people were asking if you wouldn't mind singing one of your songs for us," Denise said to Mom. "I realize I'm springing this on you, but would you possibly be willing? It would be such a gift for us."

"I'd be happy to sing," Mom said. "And maybe the girls could sing too. They did a fantastic acapella version of their song the other night at the Opry. What do you say, girls?"

"Yes, yes, yes!" Lulu said.

Maddie wished she could be so enthusiastic.

"Actually, Henry is quite capable on our piano over there," Denise said. "You're welcome to sing acapella, but if it's a song he knows, I'm sure he'd be happy to play."

Denise called over the noise of the room that today they would have a special treat. Everyone cheered. Mom and the girls took off their hairnets and aprons and went to the front of the room, where there was a small stage. The girls stood on the side of the stage while Mom conferred with Henry. Then, he played for her while she sang "You Are My All in All," standing by the piano. When she started on her second time through the chorus, Mom invited anyone in the room who knew the song to sing. Maddie's eyes teared up as many voices rose up and joined Mom's, harmonizing and filling the room with sweet music. Maddie scanned the room and found Ruby, her mom, and her little brother. They were all singing with giant smiles on their faces. The lump in Maddie's throat tightened. Ruby was just about her age, clearly loved to sing, and was like Maddie in so many ways. Except Ruby didn't have a home to live in.

Mia slipped her hand into Maddie's and squeezed. Maddie smiled back and saw that Mia's eyes were watery too. There was something about a room of people singing in spite of everything—especially singing a praise song—that filled her heart up and made it overflow. If she tried to explain what her heart was so full of, she'd say happiness and possibilities. Maybe the word was hope. Hope, when you didn't always have enough to eat, when you didn't even have a place to live . . . it was . . .

"Beautiful," Mia whispered.

"I know," Maddie agreed.

"Our turn," Lulu said, elbowing Maddie in the ribs.

Sure enough, Mom was motioning them over. She went back to Henry to tap out the tempo of their song. He launched into "This Little Light of Mine," playing with gusto.

Maddie didn't have time to be nervous. They launched into the melody, and it was mid-song before she fully realized what she was doing. By that time, she, Mia, and Lulu were completely in sync, harmonizing, and moving to the music. They caught one another's eyes every once in a while and beamed. This was . . . fun! Maddie kept right on singing through to the end of the song. The room erupted with applause. Ruby jumped to her feet with everyone else, clapping and even adding a whistle or two.

"Encore!" someone shouted.

So, Henry launched into "You Are Awesome in this Place." Mom joined the girls, and wrapped her arms around them. Everyone sang and sang, until Henry played the final chords.

Denise gave each of them giant hugs. "Thank you so much, ladies. It has been such a treat for us to have you here with us today."

"It's been a treat for us too," Mom said.

Maddie nodded. She hadn't known what to expect when they came today, but she certainly hadn't expected to leave feeling more full than when she came. Her stomach had even stopped growling, even though she still hadn't had her own lunch. It was time to go, but before she left, she caught Ruby's eye and gave her a small wave. Ruby waved back, her dimple deepening again as she smiled.

"We have to find that guitar," Mia said.

"I know," Maddie said. "We really, really have to."

Back in the front office, they bundled back into coats.

Mom said, "I'm so proud of you girls."

"Do you think we warmed their hearts?" Lulu asked. "Not just their bellies?"

At this, Maddie's stomach growled loud enough for everyone in the room to hear. They all burst out laughing.

"I think so," Mom said. "And it sounds like it's time for us to find some lunch ourselves. Everyone ready?"

"Ready!" Maddie said.

"Me too," Mia said.

"Off to lunch we go!" Lulu announced.

TWENTY

Dad met them at the stage door. "How did it go at Third Street?"

"The girls did a fantastic job, hairnets and all," Mom said. "And we gave an impromptu concert."

"How was that?" Dad asked.

"Awesome!" Lulu said, throwing her arms up to emphasize just how awesome it had been.

"How about for you, Maddie?" Dad asked. "I know you've been a little worried about Friday night."

"I had fun," she said. "Lots of fun, actually."

"Did Charles find anything on the tapes?" Mia asked. "We have to find that guitar, Dad. Did you know there are kids at the shelter? And Mom said there are people on a wait list—they don't have enough room for everyone who needs a place to stay. We have to do all we can to help."

Dad shook his head. "Unfortunately, the footage didn't give us anything to follow up on. While there were a lot of people coming in and out of the building, no one stood out as being out of place, Charles said."

"And he watched all the footage?" Mia asked. "Every single minute of it?"

"Well, like he said, there was a lot of time between when we last saw the guitar and when we discovered it missing. There are at least ten cameras around the building, so that's a lot of footage. But I believe Charles and his team did their best, Mia. We just have to pray whoever took the guitar has a change of heart."

"Maybe we should look for clues?" Mia said.

Mom put her arm around Mia. "I know you want to be detectives, but it's important for us to focus on the concert. I understand why you'd want to raise as much money as possible, girls, especially after meeting all the people at Third Street today. But your song is a gift for the benefit too. Let's put our attention on what we can do—singing our very best—and we'll pray that God will work on the heart of the person who took the guitar. Like Denise said today, God works in mysterious ways."

"Miss Julia is waiting in the Women of Country Music room for you, girls," Dad said. "You can leave your coats there, and then come out onto the stage right away so we can check our sound levels."

Maddie could see that Mia wanted to stop and ask Charles questions as they passed his desk. "Maybe we'll have time later."

"I know it's important to trust God to work things out," Mia said. "But shouldn't we also do something? It feels wrong to just hope that it will all be okay."

"Hope what will be okay?" Miss Julia asked, hearing the last of this.

"Mia wants to find the guitar," Lulu said.

"We all do," Maddie said. "Miss Julia, there was this girl at the shelter today, Ruby, and she was, I don't know . . . just like us."

"Not exactly like us." Mia pulled off her coat and draped it over a chair.

"No, but she's our age, and she likes to sing. When I think about people who don't have homes, I think about people like that man who shouted at us outside the Opry. Grown-ups. People I wouldn't know how to talk to. But Ruby was different, and I just . . . I don't know." Maddie took off her coat too, and piled both hers and Lulu's on top of Mia's.

"It's one of the reasons your mom is so passionate about the problem of homelessness, and why she hosts this benefit each year. In most American cities, the largest number of homeless people are children." Miss Julia took their coats and started to hang them up. "Actually, you girls can hang up your own coats!" She handed over hangers.

"But you never see children out on the street with cardboard signs asking for money or food," Mia said, hanging her coat on the rack.

"Usually not," Miss Julia said. "But for every homeless mom or dad, there are often two or more children who also don't have a place to live. That's why shelters like Third Street are so important. Shelters provide a place for families to stay, and for children to be safe, while parents work toward getting jobs and the ability to pay for housing and food."

"But how do they end up without jobs and home-less?" Maddie asked. "Did they do something wrong and get fired?"

"People lose their jobs for all sorts of reasons. Once, I heard a woman tell her story—she and her husband both worked in service jobs. Neither made much money, but they had enough to pay their bills from month to month and to save a little. He worked at the airport, helping load baggage onto planes, and she worked at the post office. Then, for a lot of reasons, there came a few months where many people were laid off from their jobs. First the woman lost her job, and then her husband did too."

"What does laid off mean?" Maddie asked.

"That's when a company has to cut back the number of people who work for them. People don't get laid off for doing anything wrong, but because there's not enough work and not enough money to pay them anymore."

"So what happened to the people?" Lulu wanted to know.

"They both took temporary jobs at a fast food restau-rant and worked hard, but they had to use money from their savings every month because they weren't earn-ing enough. They had to pay their rent and buy food for their three kids, who were four, six, and seven. Money got tighter and tighter, and then, one day, their boss called the whole staff in and told them the restaurant was closing."

"So, they didn't have jobs again?" Mia asked.

"Right," Miss Julia said. "But it was worse this time, because they'd used up most of their savings. They didn't have enough to live on while they looked for new jobs. So, they started selling their furniture and other possessions, until they just had one suitcase for each person. On the last night of the month, they packed the kids into the car to go to their favorite park and have a picnic dinner of peanut butter and jelly sandwiches. They let the kids play until the sun set, and then everyone loaded back into the car. And then they drove around, not knowing where to go. The kids asked their parents when they could go home and go to bed, but of course, they didn't have a house to go home to. They drove until the kids fell asleep and then they parked the car and slept. The next day, they went to apply for help at the shelter."

"Do they live at the shelter now?" Maddie asked.

"They're a success story, actually," Miss Julia said. "At the shelter, they both received training. The dad ended up getting a job at a local church, running the music program. The mom took some university courses and earned the certificate she needed to be a pre-school teacher. They moved out of the shelter, and now I believe he comes back for lunch most days to help out with music. He's a talented piano player."

"Henry!" the girls said in unison.

"You met him?" Miss Julia asked.

"He played our song for us today," Mia said.

"Thanks for telling us his story," Maddie said.

"You're welcome," Miss Julia said. "But now you girls had better hurry up and get out there on stage! I know your dad wanted to start rehearsal as soon as possible."

"Are you coming to watch?" Lulu asked.

"You bet!" Miss Julia said.

TWENTY-ONE

Finally! There you are!" Dad called from the front of the stage. "Come on over here, girls, and let's check how you sound in this microphone."

Lulu bounded across the stage, ready, as always, to have a microphone in hand. With the full band on stage, and the empty microphone waiting for them, the upcoming performance was starting to feel very, very real.

"You'll do great!" Mom said, giving Maddie's shoulder a squeeze as she passed by. "I'll be out in the auditorium so I can see everything and give you girls some direction. Have fun and embrace the moment!"

Dad arranged them with Mia in the middle. "Okay, let's check this out. Let's just sing a line or two."

While they sang, Dad stared at his feet, listening to the band and the voices together. "How's that sounding, Gloria?"

"A little louder on the microphone" she said.

Lulu bumped Mia out of the way and took center stage, standing smack-dab in the middle of the Opry circle. "I should be in the middle, because I'm the smallest!"

She stood on her tiptoes, but wasn't tall enough to reach the microphone. Mia stepped aside, but looked questioningly at Dad to see if he would let Lulu get away with this. Dad, in turn, looked out at Mom.

"Actually, it does look best with Lulu in the middle," Mom said. "But Lulu, check your heart. Remember, this isn't just your performance."

Dad brought a crate out so Lulu could stand on top and be tall enough to sing into the microphone.

"Lulu, a little quieter please," Mom said.

"So you don't drown us all out," Mia told her.

"Well, you should speak up," Lulu said. "Or sing up, or whatever."

"Maddie, I can't hear you at all," Dad said. "I know you can be louder. Send your voice out to the audience, all the way out to Mom."

"Pretend you're singing at the shelter," Mia said. "You were perfectly loud there."

Maddie glanced around the stage at all the people watching and breathed deeply. At the shelter, she hadn't felt so put on the spot. There was no microphone, and so much less pressure. Here, singing felt so much more . . . serious. She counted again, doing her best to push her voice out farther.

"Much better," Dad said. "Nice job, Maddie."

Mom nodded and smiled proudly at Maddie. "Girls, I'd like to do the version of the song where you each take a verse on your own. You sounded so great today singing the whole song together, but I'd love for you to each have your own moment to shine. When you sing your solo verse, turn the microphone so it's directed toward you, and sing directly into it. Okay?"

Behind them, the music started up, and the girls started to sing. Maddie heard her own voice bouncing back from the balcony. For a moment, this threw her off so much that she stopped singing.

Mia elbowed her and hissed, "Sing, Maddie!"

Maddie stared down at her toes. *Come on, Maddie,* she thought. *You can do this.*

It was hard to hear her harmony through the echo in the room. Everything felt off—the beat, the way her voice clashed against her sisters' voices. Mia kept using her heel to try to emphasize the beat, so they'd all be in time, but her tapping was out of sync with the drums behind them. Lulu's voice rang out louder than everything else. The more the harmonies went sour, the louder Lulu sang. She started doing fancy dance moves on her crate, as though that might distract everyone from the disaster song. Then came time for Maddie's solo. She turned the mic her way, looked down at the floor, and started to sing. As long as she didn't look out at the rows of lights, at all the empty seats, she would be fine. She tried to force herself not to listen, but she couldn't help hearing the wobbly sound in her tone, which made everything sound a little flat. Her solo seemed to go on and on, but eventually, her verse came to an end. Relieved, she turned the mic back toward Lulu.

They started singing together again for the final chorus. Lulu launched in, singing at the top of her lungs. Mia had finally had enough.

She stopped singing and said, "Lulu, knock it off!"

"We sound bad," Lulu said.

"Because you're drowning everyone out," Mia said.

"And you're bossing everyone around," Lulu said.

"Am not."

"Are too!"

The musicians stopped playing and Mom hurried up to the stage.

"We were awful," Lulu said, stamping her foot. "I want to sing again, but not with them."

"It wasn't our fault," Mia said. "If you'd stop trying to hog the whole performance, maybe we'd sound better."

"I wasn't hogging!" Lulu said.

"Girls, stop," Mom said, her face serious. She called to the band, "Hey, everyone, let's take five."

Dad came over. "Want me to stick around?"

"I'll take this one to start," Mom said.

"Right. Let me know if you need me," he said.

The girls followed Mom into the seating area. They sat on the wooden benches, looking at the empty stage. For a long moment, Mom didn't say anything at all.

"We didn't get the heart thing right, did we?" Mia asked.

Mom gave a slow, sad shake of her head. "I know it's hard, especially when you have a microphone and are on this Opry stage. But I saw you sing from your hearts—your sweet, beautiful hearts—this afternoon at the shelter. I know you can do it. We're going to try it again, and here's what I want you to think about. Maddie, I want you to look up, and take a mental picture when you sing. This is your first time singing at the Opry—it's a special moment, you should enjoy it. Okay?"

Maddie pressed her fingers into the cool wood of her seat. "Okay."

Mom gently tilted her chin up. "That means no more looking at your feet, okay?"

With Mom smiling at her like this, Maddie couldn't help but smile too. "Okay."

"Mia, it doesn't have to be perfect," Mom said. "Just do your best and have fun. If you're so busy trying to be perfect, you're going to miss the moment. The best moments are not perfect. It's about having passion in the moment."

"I can do that," Mia said. "I can try, anyway."

"Good," Mom said. "And Lulu?"

Lulu gave Mom an innocent look. "Like I said, it's not all about you. I want you thinking as much about your sisters up there as you think about yourself. And not about what your sisters should or shouldn't be doing. I want you to think about having fun with them. About enjoying this experience together. Got it?"

Lulu threw her arms around Mom in a giant hug. "Got it."

"Okay, then," Mom said. "Let's try this again."

TWENTY-TWO

After a few more run-throughs of the song, the girls hit their stride. Maddie managed to look up as she sang. Lulu pulled her voice back and tamed her dance moves. Mia made it all the way through without stopping to give instructions. Mom joined them onstage to sing backup, and the musicians worked through the final musical details. Performing with Mom behind them felt strange, but knowing she was there reassured Maddie. If anything happened, she knew Mom could guide them back to where they needed to be in the song.

Since they finished their rehearsal midafternoon, they had the rest of the night off. Ms. Carpenter had given Maddie and Mia a free night—no homework—so they could prepare for the benefit. The minute they walked in the door at home, Mia and Lulu ran upstairs to figure out their costumes. Maddie curled up on the couch, needing a little quiet time. So much had happened today, and she needed to think.

"You okay?" Mom asked, sitting down next to her on the couch.

"Yeah. I think so," Maddie said. "Well, I don't know."

Peals of laughter floated down from upstairs. Mia obviously thought that whatever Lulu wanted to wear for the concert was hilarious.

"Want to take a walk?" Mom asked.

A quiet walk with Mom sounded perfect. Maddie jumped off the couch. "Yes!"

They walked up the street to the path they sometimes walked on, through the trees and down toward the creek. The path was still wet from the rain, but the gray clouds had given way to bright blue sky. Trees lined the path, their leaves yellow, orange, and red.

"Do you think we helped today—at Third Street?" Maddie asked. "I mean, I know we served food, but I don't know . . . did we help? That girl we were talking to today, Ruby, she was our age and she liked music— she's like me and Mia. But she doesn't have a home to live in. I talked to her and everything, but that doesn't seem like much. I want to help, Mom, but what would I even do?"

Mom stopped, pointing out a deer across the field. The deer leapt toward the trees, where a spotted fawn waited.

"Instead of looking at how big the problem seems, remember that the littlest things you do can make all the difference."

"Like talking to Ruby?" Maddie asked.

"Exactly. Or like singing together. Did you see the way faces lit up when people started to sing?"

"I know they need food and somewhere to live, but like Denise said, it seems like what they actually need is . . . to believe that someday things can be different, I guess. But how do you change a person's mind?" Now Maddie wasn't only thinking about Ruby, but also about Annabeth and Emily.

They'd made it down to the creek, and Mom picked up a rock to skip across the water.

"Annabeth and Emily are mad at us," Maddie said. "You know how we made that dance, since they had one that didn't include us? Anyway, I guess making our own dance was the wrong thing to do. And then they got even more upset because we're singing at the Opry. Everything feels, I don't know. Like how things felt when we first sang our song today. Everything is off-key and out of rhythm. And I don't know how to fix it."

Mom's rock skipped once, and then twice, and she picked up another rock to try again. "Ruby, Annabeth, and Emily, plus the concert—that's a lot of challenges to be thinking about at once."

"I want to make a difference—a real difference—for Ruby. But I'm just me. What can I do?"

"The desire to want to help someone comes from God. And God seems to have put Ruby, in particular, on your heart. Is anything else on your heart, maybe about what you might do to help her?"

"I don't know. I guess I could pray for her," Maddie said.

"That's a perfect place to start," Mom said. "And while you're at it, you could also ask God to help you know what else you might be able to do."

"What if I can't tell what God is telling me to do?" Maddie said. "If we can't hear God's voice out loud, how are we supposed to know?"

"That's a great question," Mom said. "For me, the more I pray about something, the more I hear God's voice. I check in with myself and notice. Is this a desire that doesn't go away? What's that idea or thought that keeps coming back? That's the Holy Spirit nudging you."

"Could we pray right now?" Maddie asked.

"Absolutely," Mom said.

They sat on a rock. Maddie waited, listening to the stream going by, letting her mind become as quiet as it could. Then she prayed, "God, I want to do something for Ruby. Maybe to give her something. But I don't know what to give—she needs so much. I can't give her a house or a happier life, not right away. I also want to fix things with Annabeth and Emily, and I don't know how to do that either. Will you help me? Maybe give me an idea? Thank you for helping me sing today at the shelter, and also for helping me again at the Opry. Help me not to panic tomorrow night. Make it as dark as possible in the audience, God, so I can't see all those eyes. In Jesus' name, Amen."

"Amen." Mom kissed Maddie on the top of her head. "I'll pray for those things too, sweet girl. And now, what do you say we go home and see what the girls want to wear for the concert?"

"Let's do it." Maddie picked up a rock to skip. "After I skip this rock."

"Go for it," Mom said.

TWENTY-THREE

"Come see, come see, Mommy!" Lulu shouted from upstairs.

Maddie tried to picture what Lulu would have chosen to wear for the concert, but with Lulu, anything was possible.

"I'm ready too!" Mia toppled out into the hallway in silver high heels that she must have borrowed from Mom's closet. Mia was wearing her fanciest holiday dress, with velvet, satin, and sequins.

"My feet are only a few sizes smaller than yours, Mom," she said. "We need concert shoes, don't we?"

"What you need is to be able to walk across the stage without falling over." Mom shook her head, smiling. "Okay, Lulu, let's see your outfit."

"Ta-da!" Lulu threw open her bedroom door.

There she stood in her hot pink-striped bathing suit and cowboy boots. She'd found a fancy dress-up hat covered with ribbons and lace, and wore that too. It was too big, and slipped down over one of her eyes. Pushing it up again, she curtseyed low. "What do you think?"

Maddie and Mia both burst out laughing.

"What?" Lulu asked.

Mia choked out an answer over her laughter. "First of all, you can't wear a bathing suit on stage at the Opry."

"All right, girls," Mom said. "Let's find you something you can wear. Mia, that dress is much too fancy. Let's take a look in your closet."

"Maybe we should go shopping?" Maddie suggested, following Mom into Mia's bedroom.

"You have plenty of dresses to pick from." Mom rifled through Mia's dresses and pulled out a few flowered dresses in pinks, purples, greens, and yellows. She found some similar options in Maddie's closet, and then said, "Lulu, I think you have a dress that will match too. Let's go see."

Down the hallway they all traipsed and found two similar dresses in Lulu's closet. The girls tried on one combination and stood together in front of Lulu's full-length mirror. Mom nodded, looking at each of them, and then stepped back to look at all three together.

"I like it, but let's try the other ones, just to see."

They tried a couple other combinations. Maddie liked all the dresses Mom had picked out for her, but the one Mom eventually chose was the one made of the softest fabric. It was also the most comfortable to wear. Maddie's skirt flared out at her waist, and the floaty fabric made her feel like dancing. She stood with her sisters and studied their reflection.

"We don't exactly match, but we kind of do," she said.

"I like it," Mia said. "But are you sure we shouldn't wear something fancier?"

"I think you look beautiful," Mom said.

"I agree!" Dad chimed, in, coming into Lulu's room, his arms filled with boxes. Three shoeboxes, to be exact, and not just any shoeboxes, but boxes the size of cowboy boots. "I bought you a surprise, girls."

"Ooooh!" The girls rushed over to open the boxes.

He winked at Maddie as she took out her pair of silver, sparkly cowboy boots. "You needed something special for your Opry debut."

"Thank you, thank you, thank you!" Lulu barreled into Dad and threw her arms around him.

Mia and Maddie joined her in giving Dad a giant bear hug.

"Aren't you going to try them on?" he asked.

The girls sat on the bed and wrestled their feet into the new boots. When they were on, the girls lined up to look in the mirror one last time.

"So, what do you think, Lulu?" Mom asked.

"If I can't wear my bathing suit," she said, giving a little spin-kick to try out her boots, "then this is perfect."

Mia slipped her arm through Maddie's. "This is going to be so much fun!"

"Your boots fit?" Dad asked, checking each of their toes. "I don't want any sore feet tomorrow night."

Fortunately, everyone's boots fit.

"Okay, let's get you out of those dresses," Mom said. "We want to keep them nice and clean for tomorrow night."

They changed back into their regular clothes, and Mom decided they should all have some quiet time before dinner. Maddie took out her colored pencils and sketchpad. Mia curled up with her book, and Lulu went into their parents' room to read with Dad. Maddie tried to focus on her drawing, but her conversation with Mom kept rolling around in her mind.

God, help me to know what I can do for Ruby. And if there's anything I can do for Annabeth and Emily, help me see that too.

Maddie leaned back against her pillows, looking over at the closet. Mom was right, they had so many dresses to choose from. All they had to do was look in their closets, and they could easily find something to wear for a concert at the Opry. It wouldn't be that way for Ruby, not even close. Maddie wondered whether she had a closet at the shelter. Where did people keep their things? How many things would they even have? She looked around her room then, and imagined trying to pack everything important into one suitcase each. Miss Julia had said Henry's family had to travel with just one suitcase each. It must have been similar for Ruby.

TWENTY-FOUR

Maddie tiptoed into Mia's room, hoping a quiet conversation counted as quiet time. "Mia?"

"Hmm?" Mia said, still deep in her book. She'd started reading *Anne of Green Gables* a few days ago. Even though it had been so busy, she'd still managed to read almost half of the book already.

Maddie perched on Mia's bed. "If you didn't have . . . well, all the things we have here . . . like a closet full of dresses and toys and books and everything, what would you want?"

"I don't know, I suppose I'd want all those things— dresses, clothes, toys, definitely books," Mia said.

"But what if you didn't have a lot of room? Like, if you had to keep everything in one suitcase, like Henry's family?"

"I'm sure Henry's family has more room than just one suitcase each, now, Maddie. Miss Julia said they moved into their own apartment."

"Yeah." Maddie played with the fabric of Mia's comforter, rubbing it between her fingers. "But Ruby's family doesn't have their own apartment."

"True." Mia closed her book. "That's why I want to find the guitar so much. If we can raise a lot of money for the shelter, maybe we can make a difference for families like Ruby's."

"But there aren't any clues to help us find the guitar," Maddie said. "And even if there were any clues, we have hardly any time to solve the mystery."

"But we shouldn't give up," Mia said.

"No, so in the meantime, isn't there something else we can do to help Ruby?"

"Like give her some of our things?" Mia asked.

"Yes, I guess we could. But we can't walk into the shelter with our arms full of bags or boxes just for her. We'd embarrass her. Plus, there are a lot of other people there who need help too, right?"

Maddie thought about how it might feel to have someone bring you a bag of things at a place like the shelter. One time, for Valentine's Day, Emily had pressed brightly wrapped packages into Mia and Maddie's hands at the end of the day. The gifts turned out to be silver charm bracelets. Even though Maddie loved hers, she felt strange wearing it to school the next day. She hadn't given anything to Emily. It seemed that if someone gave you a gift, you should give them one in return, unless it was your birthday or something.

"It might embarrass her," Maddie admitted. "But I don't think it's right to do nothing just because we're not sure what to do."

"Yeah," Mia said. "Did you talk to Mom about it?"

"She said that sometimes the littlest thing helps," Maddie said. "I'll keep thinking about it. I'm sure there's something we can do."

"And think about the guitar too," Mia said. "What haven't we tried? I know there aren't any footprints or clues to follow, but it feels wrong to only wait and hope someone will return the guitar, doesn't it?"

"Yeah," Maddie said.

"Dinnertime, girls!" Mom called upstairs.

"Probably, we shouldn't talk about the guitar at dinner," Maddie said.

"Right," Mia said. "But I'll keep thinking."

"Me too."

The minute they finished dinner, Mia wanted to talk to Lulu and Maddie in her room. "Okay, I have an idea," she said. "We haven't talked to the people who work at the Opry, like Amanda. There are a lot of people who might have seen something suspicious."

"Wouldn't they have said something already?" Maddie flopped onto Mia's bed, feeling wrung out. She was full of problems that had no solutions. Her head hurt from thinking all through dinner and coming up with nothing.

"Said something about what?" Lulu wanted to know.

"About seeing something suspicious at the Opry." Maddie moved over to make room for Lulu on the bed.

"But what if the person didn't realize that what they saw had anything to do with the guitar?" Mia said. "Sometimes what you see isn't suspicious all by itself. But, combined with all the other suspicious things that are going on, a pattern shows up. You know, like

Jackson? No one suspected him of letting animals out of their exhibits at the water park until we noticed him showing up in lots of places he shouldn't have been."

"So maybe three people saw a stranger, like that?" Lulu asked.

"Exactly," Mia said.

"It can't hurt to ask," Maddie said.

Mia sat at her desk and took out paper and pencil. "I'll draw a map of the Opry, so we can take notes tomorrow."

"I'll help!" Lulu bounced off the bed to look over Mia's shoulder.

Maddie went back to her room, to her closet, and ran her hand across the many clothes hanging there. Somehow, there must be a way to give Ruby . . . something. Maybe not bags and bags of things, but something. Maybe their parents would let them go to the shelter tomorrow at lunch.

Maddie rushed back to Mia's room. "Maybe she can come to the concert!"

"Who?" Lulu asked.

"We have the seats Mom saved for Annabeth and Emily, and they're not coming. And Ruby loves music. She'd love the concert, wouldn't she?"

"Why aren't Annabeth and Emily coming?" Lulu asked.

"They're just not," Mia said, and Maddie felt another pang of sadness. Still, if Ruby and one of her family members could come instead, that would be something.

"We could go to Third Street tomorrow and give her something—something small—and invite her to the concert!" Maddie said. "We could tell her we need a friend in the audience, because we do. At least I do."

"It's a good idea," Mia said. "What kind of small thing would we give her? Something warm, like a coat?"

"That could work. Or mittens or a hat or something. It's going to keep getting colder," Maddie said.

"I wouldn't want a coat," Lulu said. "I'd want something to play with, like a doll."

"I'd want . . ." Maddie scanned the room, thinking. That's when she saw Mia's silver charm bracelet, the one Emily had given her, sitting on the top of her dresser. *A friend,* Maddie thought. But how do you give someone your friendship? Especially someone like Ruby, who she might not ever see again? The thing about Emily's bracelet was that whenever Maddie wore hers, she felt connected to her friend. Even now, when they were far apart in so many ways, the bracelet felt like a promise. We're connected. We're friends, even when things are difficult.

"What would you want?" Lulu asked.

Instead of answering, Maddie hurried into her room. She brought back her jewelry box and sat on Mia's floor. She sorted through the necklaces and bracelets until she found what she was looking for. A necklace with a delicate silver heart, angled to the side. She cradled the necklace in her hand.

"You can't give her that!" Lulu said. "Mom and Dad gave that to you. And it's one of your favorites!"

"It's special," Maddie said. "That's what I think I'd want. Something special. Something a friend would give to a friend."

"Well . . ." Mia said, looking doubtful. "I'm not sure Mom and Dad will let you give your necklace away."

"I think they'll understand," Maddie said.

"Girls, it's bedtime," Mom said, stopping by Mia's room. "We want you well rested for tomorrow. Let's go brush our teeth and wash our faces."

Maddie decided to wait until breakfast to run her idea past Mom. She needed to think about it a little more.

TWENTY-FIVE

Cinnamon rolls!" Lulu shouted as she bounded down the stairs.

Maddie laughed as she and Mia followed. When they weren't traveling, sometimes they had cinnamon rolls for breakfast as a special treat. Today was extra special, because not only were they at home, but tonight was the night of the Opry benefit.

"Plus bacon," Dad said. "You need your protein to make it a balanced meal."

Mom just shook her head and smiled.

"I know we're supposed to go to school today," Maddie said, sitting at the table.

"I hear a but coming," Dad said.

"Well, Mia and I thought that since Annabeth and Emily don't want to come tonight, maybe we should invite Ruby and a guest. Like her mom or someone." Maddie took a cinnamon roll, which was still warm from the oven, and breathed deeply. Cinnamon, warm sugar, a whiff of vanilla. "Mmmm."

"Pass the plate!" Lulu said.

"Me first," Mia said, which was technically fair because she was between Maddie and Lulu.

"Hmph." Lulu tapped her fingers on her plate while she waited.

"Relax, Lulu." Mia passed the plate. "There's plenty to go around."

"How many can I have?" Lulu asked.

Mom raised an eyebrow. "Let's start with one."

"We could go to the shelter today and invite her," Maddie said.

"And Maddie wants to give Ruby her heart necklace," Lulu added. "The one you gave her last year for Christmas."

"That's very sweet, honey," Mom said. "But are you sure? You love that necklace."

"I want to give her something special," Maddie said. "If I gave her a dress I didn't like anymore or something, that wouldn't be a real gift. Plus, she could wear the necklace and remember that she has friends."

"I love that idea, Maddie," Mom said.

"And I want to give her a coat and gloves," Mia said.

"And I'm giving her a doll!" Lulu said.

"All wonderful gifts," Dad said.

"So what do you say?" Maddie wanted to know. "Can we give her Annabeth and Emily's tickets?"

"Are you sure the girls don't want to come?" Mom asked. "I should call their moms and make sure before we give them away."

"Maybe they changed their minds," Mia said, exchanging a look with Maddie. "But I doubt it."

"I'm sure things will work out between you girls," Mom said. "It's hard, sometimes, when a friend has an

opportunity you wish you could have. But jealous feelings don't last forever."

"I wish jealous feelings went away faster," Maddie
said. "I really want Annabeth and Emily to come tonight.
But if Ruby can come instead, that makes it a little better.
At least I'll have one friend in the audience."

"You'll have lots of friends in the audience," Mom
said. "Ms. Carpenter, for one, and lots of our family
friends. But I understand what you mean. You want
someone who's there especially for you."

"So can we go to the shelter today?" Maddie asked.
"Please, Mom?"

"I didn't want you to miss another day of school,"
Mom said. "But a low-key day is important, so maybe
it will be better this way. I'll call Ms. Carpenter and
talk with her about schoolwork, and also check in with
Annabeth and Emily's moms, just in case."

The girls finished their cinnamon rolls and bacon
and went upstairs to collect their gifts for Ruby.
Soon, Mom came upstairs and peeked her head into
Maddie's room.

"Come with me to Mia's room, okay?"

Maddie latched the heart necklace around her own
neck for the last time and followed Mom. A knot tightened in her stomach . . . Was something wrong? Mom
went first to Lulu's room and explained she needed a
few minutes to talk with Maddie and Mia alone.

"Without me?" Lulu wailed.

"I promise we're not leaving you out," Mom said. "And after we've talked, you and I can pack your bag for tonight together. Maybe we can find something sparkly for you to wear in your hair."

"Okay," Lulu mumbled, clearly not sold on the plan.

"Let's sit." Mom motioned to the bed once they were alone in Mia's room with the door closed.

Maddie pulled a pillow into her lap when she sat down, hugging it to her chest.

"Are we in trouble?" Mia asked, echoing Maddie's thoughts.

"No," Mom said. "I just spoke to Annabeth and Emily's moms. They each said almost the same thing— the girls are upset, and they've both insisted they don't want to go to the concert."

"It's not fair." Mia punched her pillow. "We didn't do anything wrong, Mom, I promise we didn't."

Mom nodded. "I understand you didn't mean to hurt your friends. But most of the time when feelings are hurt, it's not a one-sided problem."

"It started when we showed them our dance," Maddie said. "I don't think we should have suggested a dance-off."

"But they started it, by making a dance that didn't leave room for us," Mia said.

"What happened after the dance-off?" Mom asked.

"We didn't even have it, because Ms. Carpenter couldn't judge it that day at recess. So, we showed them our dance, and then they went off and practiced their own dance. Without us," Mia said.

"We told them about the concert," Maddie said.

"Which didn't help. I mean, they knew about the benefit and were planning to come with us. When we told them we might be singing instead of just watching from the audience, Annabeth wasn't happy."

"Shouldn't they be happy for us?" Mia asked. "They're our best friends."

"I can see you're upset," Mom said. "And I understand why the situation doesn't feel fair to you. I wonder if you can put yourself in their shoes, though. Especially Annabeth's shoes. You know how much she loves to sing and perform. She would love to be the one up there on the stage performing. It may not be possible for her to cheer you on right now, since you're having an opportunity to do something she'd like to do so much."

"So what are we supposed to do?" Maddie asked. "I don't want them to be mad at us forever."

"How did you leave things?" Mom asked.

"They said they wanted space until after the concert," Mia said.

"Maybe you give them space, then," Mom said. "And look for a way to invite them to be part of your lives too. Maybe not for the benefit, but I'm sure something else will come up. When they see you reaching out and not holding on to your anger, it will be easier for them to let go of theirs."

"It's not fair," Maddie said. "Since we didn't do anything wrong."

"No," Mom said. "But if you look at it from their point of view, the situation isn't all that fair, either. Watching your best friends do something as exciting as singing at the Opry—leaving you behind a little bit—is difficult. When something comes between friends like this, one side or the other has to reach out to close the gap. If you wait for them to do it, you might be waiting a long time."

"I don't want that," Maddie said.

"No, I don't want that for you either," Mom said. "When the concert is over, I'm sure you'll figure out a way to reconnect."

"So, is it okay for us to invite Ruby to the show instead?" Maddie asked.

"Yes," Mom said. "And I love that we can find something good in this hard situation. Now, why don't you two finish getting ready? We'll go straight to the theater from the shelter. Miss Julia will bring your bags, so make sure you pack up everything you want for tonight."

Mom headed off to help Lulu pack, but Mia stopped Maddie before she left the room.

"Hey, Mads?" she said. "I'm sorry if I made the fight with Annabeth and Emily worse. You know, by suggesting the dance-off and everything."

"You were trying to help me," Maddie said. "You knew my feelings were hurt. Like Mom said, we'll find a way to fix this after the concert. And I'm excited that we get to invite Ruby."

"Yeah, me too," Mia said. "Things are starting to work out already. Maybe we'll even find the guitar tonight."

"Maybe." Maddie was on her way out the door when she turned back, remembering. "Don't forget to pack your map of the Opry!"

"Good call!" Mia said.

TWENTY-SIX

When they rounded the corner onto Broadway, they saw a small group gathered around a man. He sat on an overturned milk crate, playing guitar. Maddie didn't have a clear view of the man, but his music made her stop in her tracks. Lots of people played on the street, but not many were this good.

"He's talented," Mom said, noticing too.

As the man finished his song, he called out, "Feel free to toss a tip into the case, there. Don't be shy."

His voice sounded vaguely familiar, but Maddie couldn't place it.

"Should we give him a tip?" Lulu asked.

Mom dug in her purse and pulled out a few dollars. "Here, girls, why don't you each go put a dollar in his case, and then come right back."

Maddie hung back and let Mia and Lulu go first. The man was loud, and Maddie wasn't sure what to expect as they approached his open case.

"Thank you, ladies," he said, as first Lulu and then Mia dropped their dollars into the case. Maddie was about to put hers in too, when she looked up and got a good look at his face, at his scraggly beard and his blue-and-maroon hat. The pieces fell into place—his voice, his face . . .

She hurried after Mia and caught her arm. "That's the man we saw outside the Opry. The one who shouted at us about the guitars."

"Are you sure?" Mia eyed him. "I mean, they're similar, but . . ."

Mom was already around the corner, holding the door open. "Girls?"

Maddie's hand went to her neck, feeling for the necklace one more time. Would Ruby like it? She hadn't thought so back home, but now that she was here, she realized giving the necklace would be harder than giving a coat or gloves. When you offer friendship, you have to put yourself out there. The other person might not accept the gift.

"Are you sure you want to give her your necklace?" Mia asked.

"Yes," Maddie said. "Oh, yes, I definitely do, it's just that . . . what if she doesn't want it?" She didn't ask the real question: What if she doesn't want me to be her friend?

"She'll love it," Mia said.

They took off their coats, but Mia didn't hang hers up. She draped it over her arm, with the gloves stuffed in the pocket, to give to Ruby.

"Ready?" she said to Maddie and Lulu.

"Ready!" Lulu said, giving her doll one last hug.

Lulu had surprised Maddie by choosing one of her special dolls, one she liked a lot, rather than one of the more worn-out ones. But all three sisters seemed to agree. A gift should be special—whether a person had more than they needed or hardly anything at all.

Other people were in charge of the line today, and they'd come just a little later too. Most everyone had taken food back to their seats. Mom waved at Denise as they came in. She nodded, obviously expecting them. Maddie spotted Ruby, and was happy to see there was room next to her on the bench. Maddie pointed Ruby out to her sisters.

Mia grabbed Lulu's arm as she started to take off across the room. "Remember . . . casual, Lulu. We don't want to embarrass her."

Lulu shook Mia's hand off. "I know."

Still, she took the lead across the room. Maddie couldn't help smiling. Lulu may have thought she was being low-key, but her sneaking drew attention.

"Hey, are you girls back to sing?" a man called.

"Not today," Mia said.

"Tonight's the night of the benefit," someone else called. "They have to save their voices."

Finally, they made it across the room and sat next to Ruby. Once they sat down, Maddie could relax. Now, it didn't feel so much like she had a spotlight following her across the room.

"Hey!" Ruby said, clearly excited to see them. "What are you doing here?"

"We have two extra tickets for the show tonight." Maddie decided to start with the easy part. "And we wanted to see if you and someone else, maybe your mom, would want to come."

"To your concert?" Ruby's eyes went round, and she reached out for her mom's arm. "Could we?"

"I'd have to see if Dad could watch Sam," her mom said. "And you know how he feels about coming into the shelter."

"But you saw the way he was today—with the guitar. Don't you think he'd be . . . He's back, isn't he, Mom?" Ruby said.

Rather than answering, Ruby's mom pressed her lips together and looked down at her hands. When she finally looked up, Maddie could tell she was choosing her words carefully. "I don't want you to be disappointed, Ruby. Let's wait until I talk to Dad before we make a final decision." She then turned to the girls and smiled a sad kind of smile. "Girls, thank you so much for thinking of us. If there's any way we can come, we definitely will."

"Did you see Dad outside, playing the guitar?" Ruby asked the girls, once her mom was distracted, helping Sam with the butter and his roll. "A whole crowd is out there listening. Ever since Dad had to sell his guitar, it was like he sold a part of himself. But now that he has a guitar, he's back. He's back and things will be better now."

"Wait," Maddie said. "That's your dad outside?"

"Yes!" Ruby said. "So, you heard him?"

"He's really good," Mia said, and then nudged Maddie. Across the room, Mom was motioning for them. Time to go.

Maddie took a deep breath, and then plunged in. She unclasped the necklace from around her neck, cupped it in her hand, and then pressed it into Ruby's palm. "For you," she said.

It hardly seemed possible for Ruby to look more shocked than she had when they'd invited her to the concert, but she did now. She stared at the necklace in her palm, and then in what seemed like slow motion, she smoothed the chain so she could see the delicate chain and heart.

"Thank you," she said, and then looked Maddie directly in the eyes. "Thank you."

Maddie could see that Ruby understood about the gift—that it wasn't just a necklace, but something more. She felt light enough to float up off the bench. "Lulu and Mia have something for you too!"

Lulu and Mia handed over the doll, coat, and gloves. Ruby threw her arms around each of the girls in turn. "Thank you, thank you, thank you!"

"And I also brought you a story," Lulu said. "I wrote it myself!"

"Girls, we can't thank you enough," Ruby's mom said from across the table, having finished with Sam's roll and catching the end of what had just happened. "If there's any way that we can come to the concert tonight, I promise we will."

"They'll have tickets at will-call under your name," Mia said. "And Mom will pay for a taxi to drive you there and back. She said she'd leave some money with Denise for you."

Maddie squeezed Ruby's hand. "I hope you can come! I could really use a friend in the audience."

Ruby squeezed back. "Even if I'm not there, I'll be thinking about you." She let go and touched the neck-lace, which she'd already clasped around her own neck. "I promise."

TWENTY-SEVEN

O ff we go," Mom said from the front seat. "Buckle up, girls."

"Now we need to think of something to give to Sam!" Lulu buckled her seat belt. "Maybe a stuffed animal?"

"Maybe," Maddie said, distracted.

"Where do you think Ruby's dad got a guitar?" Mia asked.

Maddie didn't dare meet Mia's eyes. She'd been wondering that too. Guitars weren't cheap. If her dad had sold his guitar for money before, he wouldn't have suddenly had the money to buy a new one. Near the shelter, a lot of people sat on the street and played, cases open, to earn some money. "Maybe someone loaned it to him?"

"Mmmm," Mia said.

"Sam would like my stuffed elephant," Lulu said. "I know he would!"

"Ruby's mom said they had to ask her dad about watching Sam," Maddie told Mom. "I hope he will, so they can come."

"I hope so too." Mom smiled into the mirror, catching Maddie's eye. "How did Ruby like your gifts?"

"She loved them!" Lulu bounced in her seat. "When I gave her the doll, she gave it a big hug. And I think she'll like my story too. It's the complete adventures of Featherwing, the fairy."

"You added to the story?" Maddie asked.

Lulu launched into a description of what she'd added, plus what she planned to add next. Maddie tried to follow the complex twists and turns of the mystery.

"You're pretty quiet back there, Mia," Mom said, after a while. "Everything okay?"

"Mmm," Mia said again.

Maddie gave her a questioning look, but Mia shook her head. Now wasn't the time to share. The drive rushed by, and soon they were just around the corner from the Opry. Maddie's skin prickled with goose bumps. Even now, she couldn't picture herself walking out on stage in front of all those people. Whether she could picture it or not, it would happen tonight, before they got back into the car to go home. Mom rounded the corner into the parking lot and drove past the mall.

"Miss Julia will meet us here—she's bringing your costumes. We'll rehearse your song around four, but for the next couple hours you can hang out in the dressing rooms, eat a snack, and rest."

"Do you need any help?" Maddie asked.

"Thank you, sweetheart," Mom said. "That's very thoughtful. But I think we've got everything covered. I'm meeting with the auction committee to talk through last details, and then we'll do a sound check and final rehearsal with the band. I'd like for you girls to take it easy so you're fresh and ready for tonight."

Miss Julia met them at the stage door. "Girls, you'll never guess what just came for you in the dressing room!"

"Ooh!" Lulu shouted, running ahead to see.

"Slow down, Lulu," Mom called, but her smile told Maddie she knew exactly what waited in the dressing room. "I'll see you girls in a little bit. Remember, rehearsal at four, and no need to put on your costumes until after."

"Okay!" Maddie threw her arms around Mom. "And thank you!"

"For what?" Mom asked innocently.

"Come on!" Maddie grabbed Mia's arm and pulled her down the hall.

The dressing room was full of flowers. Pink and yellow roses filled three matching vases. There were two other vases too. One with every shade of pink Gerbera daisies that Maddie had ever seen, and the other filled with sunflowers.

"The roses are from Mom and Dad!" Lulu held up a white card she'd pulled out of the envelope labeled "Lulu."

"Maddie," Mia said, frowning over the card in her hand, pulled from the vase of sunflowers. "Look at this."

"What's wrong?" Maddie asked.

Mia handed over the card, and Maddie read, "You'll be awesome tonight, I know it. Love, Emily."

Maddie looked at Mia, blinking tears away. A slow smile spread across Mia's face, and neither of them had to say anything at all. Maybe their best friends wouldn't be there tonight, but soon things would be back to normal.

Miss Julia came in then and started unpacking a snack.

"The daisies are from you!" Mia said, reading the final card. "Thank you, Miss Julia!"

"You're welcome!" Miss Julia said.

"I came up with more to add to my story," Lulu said. "Can I write it right now?"

"Absolutely." Miss Julia dug in her bag for paper, a pencil, and colored pencils.

"We'll be right back!" Mia seized the opportunity and grabbed Maddie's arm, dragging her out into the hall.

"What's going on?" Maddie asked.

"So, I've been thinking about the security video," Mia said. "Charles and the guards didn't see any-thing, but what if we watched the footage? We might see something they didn't. Haven't we been saying all along that the reason we should try to solve the mystery is because we see things that other people don't? So, shouldn't we watch the tapes?"

"But Mia, even if we see something, it's too late," Maddie said. "The benefit is tonight! There's no way we'd find whoever it was that took it and get the guitar back in time. Plus, remember? There's hours of footage."

"Just come with me," Mia pleaded. "Please, Maddie? We can just watch a little bit of the footage, and see what we see. Don't we have to at least try?"

Maddie knew what Mia was thinking and not saying. Ruby's dad having a guitar after they'd seen him outside the Opry felt like too much of a coincidence. "Should we tell Miss Julia?"

"We can go ask at the security desk, and if Charles says yes, then we'll tell her. She'll be okay with it," Mia said. "Especially if we find the thief, right? Everyone will be so happy if we find him."

"Or her," Maddie added. She really, really didn't want Ruby's dad to be the thief.

"You're thinking what I'm thinking," Mia said. "Right?"

"No," Maddie said, but they both knew that wasn't true.

"He's always wearing that blue-and-maroon knit cap," Mia said. "We could ask Charles if he saw anyone like that on the tapes, and maybe we can . . ."

"I don't like this," Maddie said.

"No," Mia said. "I know. I don't either. But, Maddie, we have to find the guitar, don't you think?"

Maddie nodded and followed Mia to the security desk.

"Hi there, girls," Charles said.

"We have a question," Mia said. "You know how you watched all the footage, looking for someone with the guitar?"

"Didn't see a thing," Charles said. "Lots of people in and out, but no one caught on camera with the guitar, unfortunately."

"Did you see anyone with a knit cap—a blue-and-maroon one?" Mia asked. "With not-so-clean hair that pokes out from the bottom of the hat like a fringe around his neck?"

"Actually, yeah. There was one guy like that. One of the band crew. He rolled in some equipment and rolled some other stuff out to the loading dock," Charles said.

Mia elbowed Maddie. "Do you remember when it was?"

Charles was already typing numbers into his computer, pulling up the video footage. He fast-forwarded and rewound, until he found what he was looking for. "There, like I said, a crew member."

Maddie felt like the floor was falling out from under her. It was Ruby's dad's hat, all right. The man was definitely not a crew member, though she could see why the guard had thought so. Ruby's dad pushed one of the big rolling boxes the crew used for cords and connectors past the camera. Charles fast-forwarded to footage a few minutes later, when the man pushed a box back toward the loading dock.

Maddie grabbed Mia's hand and squeezed it, warning her not to say anything. Mia gave her a questioning look.

"Umm . . . thank you," Maddie said.

Charles shrugged. "Sure. You bet."

"That was him," Mia said, as soon as they were out of Charles' earshot.

"Mia, we can't be sure," Maddie said. "Plus, we didn't see him with the guitar. Maybe he didn't actually take it."

Mia gave her a "come on, seriously?" look.

"If we accuse him of stealing the guitar, he'll for sure get in trouble. No one will believe his side of the story. It's not just about solving the puzzle, Mia. This is serious—real life." Maddie thought of what it felt like to watch Aria, the art thief she'd discovered in London, being snapped into handcuffs. All the fun of solving the mystery—the feeling of putting things right—had disappeared. Even though Maddie knew people had to face consequences, it wasn't any fun watching a person's freedom being taken away. "He'll probably go to jail, and then what will happen to Ruby and her family?"

Mia stared at her feet, and then finally said, "I like Ruby too, Mads, but we can't keep something like this a secret. He stole a really valuable guitar. One that could help lots of people, not just him."

"All I'm saying is that we don't know he stole it," Maddie said. "Please, can't we wait until tomorrow to talk about this with Mom and Dad? After the concert is over?"

Mia blew out a deep, frustrated breath. "Okay. But tomorrow, we have to say something."

Maddie gave her sister a giant, relieved hug. "Thank you, Mia."

TWENTY-EIGHT

The rest of the afternoon sped by. Between rehearsal, eating a picnic dinner in their dressing room, and putting on their costumes, Maddie hardly had any time to think about the guitar. Then, at six thirty, Mom and Dad came backstage to give the girls pre-show hugs.

"Remember," Mom said, holding Maddie at arm's length and looking her directly in the eyes. "I'm so proud of you, no matter what. When you're out there on stage, look up, take a mental picture, and enjoy the moment."

"It's our Opry debut!" Lulu shouted, doing yet another version of her signature spin-kick move.

"I know you're going to sparkle out there," Dad said.

"Because Glimmer girls sparkle and shine," Mia said.

"But most of all, they are kind!" Maddie and Lulu added.

"Speaking of kindness," Mom said. "The box office sent up word that Ruby and her mom are here for the show."

Maddie couldn't help but do a little leap of her own. Like Lulu, she was way too excited to stand still.

"You can sit with Miss Julia in the wings," Mom said. "And then, when I announce you, come out to your microphone." Mom raised her eyebrows at Lulu. "Exactly the way we rehearsed it. Got it?"

Lulu gave a little salute. "Got it."

Mom kissed the tops of each of their heads and Dad squeezed them tight, and then it was time. They followed Miss Julia out into the wings, behind the curtains where they could see the band, but not the audience. Blue and purple light streamed across the stage. Mom stepped out onto the stage and the crowd burst into applause. Maddie's legs bounced all on their own. Her hands fluttered together and apart and together again. The music began, so loud and full of energy that it seemed to add another color to the streams of light filling the air. Unlike during school performances, they didn't have to worry about being quiet backstage. They could have shouted to one another and no one would have heard them. No one seemed to want to talk though, not even Lulu.

They listened and watched as Mom sang and the band played. After a set of energetic songs that made Maddie want to dance, Mom slowed down and sang a few quieter songs. She didn't play Maddie's favorite song, the one she'd written especially for the girls. Mom was saving that for just before they sang. She showed a slideshow about the shelter just before intermission. Then, Mom sent everyone out into the lobby for one last chance to bid on the auction items. Now that there wasn't the guitar to bid on, the biggest item was a banjo

that belonged to Winthrop Williams. Winthrop was
another of the first musicians to play for the Opry. Since
Winthrop had played at least fifty different banjos in his
lifetime, his banjo wasn't as rare as Earl Eldridge Jr.'s
guitar. Still, the banjo was a special instrument with
history.

Mom and Dad checked on the girls during intermission but couldn't stay long because they needed to
mingle in the lobby and help with the auction. Soon,
they were back, and it was time for the second half of the
concert. Mom announced the auction was closed. She'd
announce winners at the end of the show, along with the
most-important announcement, the one they were all
waiting for—the amount of money the benefit had raised.
Everyone cheered at this, excited and hopeful.

Please, let us meet our goal, Maddie prayed. Even
without the guitar. If they'd told their parents about
Ruby's dad and the guitar, would they have it already?
She'd been sure it was too late this afternoon, but now,
she wondered if she'd been wrong. Maybe Ruby's dad
was outside the Opry playing right now. Ruby had said
this was his favorite place to play. He might not have
stolen the guitar, she reminded herself. Probably he
had, though. Even though Maddie didn't want to admit
it, Mia was right—the timing seemed like too much of a
coincidence to mean anything else.

Maddie was so busy thinking, she missed hearing
Mom start their special song.

Mia took Maddie's hand. "You ready?"

Maddie swallowed hard. Not really. But here they were, waiting in the wings. They were about to have their Opry debut. She expected her legs to go watery the way they had the other night, but something strange happened as she thought about walking across the stage and facing that audience—that audience with Ruby and her mom in it. Her muscles tightened, she took a deep breath, and she felt herself opening up to the experience. Her body buzzed with excitement as she stood up, stretched out her fingers, and stepped forward. *I'm doing this,* she thought, and then grinned. *I'm doing this!*

"I have a special treat for you," Mom said, gesturing toward the wings. "My beautiful Glimmer girls!"

Mia went first, then Lulu and then Maddie, right out into the stage lights. Maddie let the sound of the audience's applause and cheering wrap around her and pull her along. She and her sisters stepped into the Opry circle, and Mom backed up to give them the stage as she joined the band.

And then, the girls sang, each Glimmer girl stepping to the middle to sing their special solo.

Everything Maddie had pictured about the moment—the fear, the nervousness, the faces staring at her—none of that was anything like the actual moment. The actual moment was blue and purple lights, the beating of the drum vibrating through her chest, harmonies lifting up

to the rafters, the Opry lights shining down on smiling faces and hands clapping along. The stage lights were bright, but Maddie could still see out into the audience. She knew where Ruby's seats should be, right in the middle of the first row of the first balcony. There she was, leaning forward, clapping, her face full of joy. Maddie turned toward the microphone for her solo. Even then, even when it was just her voice rising above the melody from the band, she felt secure and solid, held up by invisible hands. *I am with you.* Words that could only have come from God rose up in her heart.

The song rose to its climax and then came to an end. Maddie breathed deeply, catching her breath, beaming as the audience leapt to their feet and cheered. The benefit committee came out on stage to join them. The girls moved aside so that Mom could announce the winners of the various auction items. The audience hooted and hollered for each name. Then, with a smile, the benefit committee chair handed Mom a paper that listed the total amount raised.

"We raised $150,000," Mom said. "That's $25,000 over our goal! And such needed funds to help the homeless shelter and its residents. Thank you."

The audience burst into renewed applause as the band played an all-instrument, drum-filled version of "I've Got a River of Life." Everyone danced their way off stage, high-fiving one another and celebrating. Mom and Dad swept the girls into a giant group hug.

"That was . . ." Mom said, searching for the words.

"Awwwwwesome!" Lulu finished for her, drawing the word out as everyone bubbled over with happy laughter.

And it had been, Maddie thought, while being swept along in the excitement, through the wings and back into the dressing rooms to pack up and go home. It had been awesome.

TWENTY-NINE

Maddie tossed and turned under her comforter. The more she tried to push herself into sleep, the more awake she felt. When she closed her eyes, all she could see were Ruby's deep brown eyes, the way they had danced and sparkled, lit with happiness as she talked about her dad and his guitar. *Ever since he had to sell his guitar, it was like he sold a part of himself. But now, he's back. He's back and things will be better now.*

She and Mia had agreed to talk to Mom and Dad the next day, but Maddie couldn't wait any longer. She'd wanted more time, hoping there would be some other explanation for Ruby's dad messing around with boxes at the Opry, acting like a crew member. But the harder she tried to convince herself that he hadn't stolen the guitar, the more sure she was of his guilt. The truth, and the fact that she'd kept their discovery from her parents, burned so hot inside her that she had to do something, say something. Now.

She slipped out of bed, tiptoed out the door, down the hallway, and into her parents' room.

"Mom?" she whispered, gently shaking Mom's shoulder.

Mom's eyes flew open, and her forehead creased in immediate concern. "What is it, sweetheart?"

Mom sat up to make room for Maddie to crawl into bed beside her, and then wrapped her up in the covers.

"Maddie, are you okay?" Dad asked, sitting up too.

Maddie took a deep breath, and then words started to tumble out. "When we got to the Opry today, Mia and I thought we should check the security footage ourselves, just to be sure about the guitar, and when we did, we saw Ruby's dad inside the Opry."

Mom shook her head. "I don't understand, sweetheart. We don't know Ruby's dad, only her mom."

"He's the man who shouted at us about the guitars," Maddie explained, and then turned to Dad. "Remember that man you talked to when we first took the auction items into the Opry?"

"But what does that have to do with the guitar going missing?" Mom said. "He could have been in the Opry for all kinds of reasons."

"Yes, but Ruby told us he just got a guitar—this week. Later, we saw the video of him in the Opry, pushing around crates like he was part of the crew, but he's not part of the crew, and I just . . . I don't want him to get in trouble."

"Oh, sweetheart," Mom said, squeezing her tight. "When did you and Mia see this? How long have you been worrying all on your own?"

"Just earlier tonight," Maddie said. "And I know we should have told you as soon as we saw him in the video, but I wanted Ruby to come to the concert, and

we figured it was too late to find him and get the guitar
back. At least, I thought it was. I'm . . . I'm sorry."

Mom kept her arms tightly wrapped around Maddie.
With each breath, Maddie relaxed a little more. The
guilty feeling started to fade. She'd told her parents,
and now they could fix this problem together.

"What do you think, Jack?" Mom asked.

"It sounds like we need to at least try to find this
man," Dad said. "Would we have any way to do that?"

"Ruby said he likes to play outside the Opry,"
Maddie said. "He wishes he could play on stage, and
back when he had his own guitar, that's where he
always played."

"So, I suppose we can go by the Opry tomorrow,"
Mom said. "And see if he's there. We can also let the
guards know to be looking for him. Plus, I can ask at
the shelter. His family is there, so it's likely he'll show
up every once in a while."

"But will he get in trouble?" Maddie asked.

"Stealing is a serious crime," Mom said. "But we
can absolutely listen to his side of the story. It's still
possible the guitar he has isn't the one we lost."

"Maybe," Maddie said, but she wasn't holding out
much hope.

"We can't do anything about this until morning,
though," Mom said. "And you've had a huge night. Do
you think you can go back to sleep?"

"I think so," Maddie said. "Now that I told you."

"I know that right now it seems like things won't turn out well at all," Dad said. "But God works in mysterious ways, don't forget."

"That's what Denise said," Maddie said. "At the shelter when Mom told her about the guitar."

Mom kissed Maddie's cheek. "Run off to bed, now, sweet girl. See you in the morning."

"'Night, Mom. 'Night, Dad."

"Sweet dreams, Maddie," Dad said.

Maddie crept back down the hallway to bed, feeling much better, but still not sure she'd be able to sleep. As she climbed into bed, she silently prayed. *Please, God, help Ruby, and her mom and brother, and her dad too. And if there's anything I can do to help, please show me.* She closed her eyes and let her head sink back against the pillows. *And thank you for being with me tonight, and for helping me to be brave.*

THIRTY

Lulu was Opry'd out, so she stayed with Miss Julia while Maddie and Mia went to the Opry to look for Ruby's dad. He wasn't anywhere. Mom called over to the shelter, but neither Ruby nor her mom had seen Ruby's dad that day. Maddie clenched and unclenched her fists. What if Ruby's dad took off with the guitar, leaving his family behind? She wished all over again that she had said something as soon as she and Mia had seen the footage.

They went through the side door and through to the security desk. Thankfully, it was Charles on duty again. Dad explained what Maddie and Mia had seen.

"So, that's what all those questions were about yesterday." Charles gave the girls a wry grin.

"I'm sorry we didn't tell you," Maddie said. "Mia would have, but I didn't want him to get in trouble."

"The man's family is staying at Third Street Community House," Dad said. "And the girls have become friends with his daughter, Ruby. Of course, they're hoping we can resolve this without bringing in the police, but I don't know."

Charles flipped through camera views on his security monitors. "Wait a second," he said, stopping and zooming in, magnifying the view of the steps outside the Opry. "Is this the guy?"

They all crowded around the screen, but Maddie didn't have to look very closely to recognize that tell-tale hat.

"That's him! That's him!" Mia pointed at the screen. "And he has the guitar!"

She started for the door, but Dad caught her arm. "Slow down there, kiddo. We have no idea how he'll react when we approach him about this."

"Oh." Mia considered this. "Right."

"If you don't want to call the police, we can give it a go," Charles said to Dad. "You and I can ask him to come in to talk and see how he reacts. If he tries to take off, I'm authorized to detain him. Then, we can call for help if we need it."

"Jack, I don't want you putting yourself in danger," Mom said.

Dad watched the screen for a moment. Ruby's dad tilted his head down to listen as he tuned the strings, one by one.

"He's a musician," Dad said. "I can try talking to him that way, musician to musician. Father to father."

Mom studied the screen too, and then nodded. "Okay. But, if anything happens, please let him go. We can find him again, and even if we don't, no guitar—no matter how valuable—is more important than you."

She gave Dad a kiss. Mia, Maddie, and Mom watched the screen closely as Dad and Charles went out to the steps. The plan was they'd bring Ruby's dad into an office right off the front lobby, as long as he was willing to come with them and talk.

Maddie held her breath. On the screen, Dad approached Ruby's dad. She couldn't hear what he was saying, but Dad gave a friendly wave and approached. Charles circled around to the other side, putting himself directly in the path of where Ruby's dad might try to run. As they talked, Maddie saw Ruby's dad glance to his left and right, like a trapped animal. He looked down at the guitar, and then looked over his shoulder, spotting Charles. This was the moment. *Don't run,* she silently begged. *Don't run!* She knew if he ran, they'd have to call the police. Also, they might lose the guitar, unless he left it behind to make it easier to run.

Both Dad and Charles took one step closer. Ruby's dad lifted his hands, a clear "hey, I don't want any trouble" sign. Charles motioned for Ruby's dad to go inside the Opry. Dad placed the instrument in its case, closed and latched it, and took it along.

"I wish we could hear what they were saying," Mia said.

"Me too," Maddie said, letting her breath go, finally. "At least it looks like everyone is okay."

They sat at the desk for a while, waiting, wondering. No one had much to say. Mom stood up every once in a while to pace, and then sat down again. Finally, Dad came through the side door with the guitar in hand. They pounced on him.

"What did he say?" Maddie asked.

Dad handed the guitar over to Mom. "E. E. Jr.'s guitar, safe and sound. It was pretty weathered before it was stolen, but from what I can see, it's in the same condition as it was."

"I can't wait to call Jennifer and let her know." Mom's smile was almost as bright as it had been last night when she'd announced that they'd raised $150,000 for the shelter.

"What did he say?" Mia echoed Maddie's earlier question.

"Well, he came into the studio, saw the various instruments, and then the guitar. It's pretty beat up, and he thought—all those guitars, no one will miss just one, especially such a beat-up one."

"He had no idea of the guitar's value?"

"Doesn't appear he did," Dad said. "And honestly, I believe him. Seemed like less of a crime to him, since he thought he was walking off with a guitar no one cared about. He'd lost his own guitar—sold it, actually—to help pay the rent after he lost his job. But eventually, they'd sold all there was to sell, and his family moved into the shelter."

"That story matches what I heard from Denise about Ruby's family," Mom said.

"Yep," Dad said. "Like I said, I think he's telling us the truth. Charles is doing some paperwork, and will check to see if there's any other criminal history. If not, we don't think it's worth reporting. We have the guitar back. It's too late to auction it off, but I'm sure Jennifer will find another great cause. Maybe she'll even trust us to auction it at next year's benefit."

"Does Charles need us to stay?" Mom asked.

"I'd like to check in on him before we leave, but I think he can take things from here."

They walked around the building toward the front lobby, Mom carrying the guitar. As they came around the corner, Charles was holding the front door of the Opry open, and Ruby's dad was on his way out.

"You win some and you lose some," Ruby's dad called to Dad. "But thank you, sir, for listening and for believing me."

"What will you do now?" Maddie called after him, as he turned to go. She thought of what Ruby had said, about him coming back to life because of the guitar.

"S'pose I'll do what I always do," Ruby's dad said, shrugging a shoulder. "Find a way to survive."

Maddie watched him go, knowing that he couldn't keep the guitar, and wishing he could, all the same. He'd been able to play and earn money with the guitar. Maybe not a lot, but something. And the money he made must feel like his own—he'd earned it, after all. She thought of the homeless people she'd seen with cardboard signs, nothing to offer except outstretched hands. Being able to play must have changed everything—if only for a moment. No wonder he'd been more himself with the guitar than without it.

"Feels pretty terrible," Mia said.

"I know," Maddie said.

"At least the guitar is back," Mia said. "And maybe something good will still come from all this. I hope so."

"Me too," Maddie said.

She couldn't go back to her regular life, knowing Ruby's dad had come back to himself for a day or two, and then, in the end, lost himself again. She determined, then and there, to come up with a plan. *God, show me what I can do*, she prayed.

THIRTY-ONE

The minute they got home, Lulu wanted to hear the whole story. It wasn't the usual kind of story, the kind that felt finished when the telling was over. The guitar was back—sure—but the mess was still just as messy.

"I know it's hard, Maddie," Mia said. "But, we raised $150,000 for the shelter last night. Plus, Ruby came to the concert. And Ruby's dad didn't have to go to jail or anything. That's better than it could have been, don't you think?"

"Yeah, I guess so." Maddie felt like a gray cloud in the middle of everyone else's happiness. "I think I'll go draw for a little while."

"You sure?" Mia asked. "We could make up another dance, or go play in the backyard."

"You're tired." Mom rubbed Maddie's back. "I don't think you slept well last night."

"Play with me!!" Lulu begged Mia. "I want to go in the backyard."

Maddie dragged her exhausted body upstairs, but she didn't think she could sleep. Not right away, anyway. She took out her sketchbook and started to draw. After a few strokes, she realized she was drawing her room. Sometimes, especially when she was tired, she didn't try to come up with anything interesting to draw.

Instead, she drew what was right there, in front of her eyes. She drew her nightstand, and on it the lamp, and the pile of books. On top of the books, she drew her quarter from their performance on Monday. She worked on the quarter's round lines, and then started shading it in silver. Then, she stopped, pencil in midair, as her thoughts clicked into place.

Ruby's dad needed a guitar, but even more than that, he needed to feel valued. He wanted to take care of himself and his family. He wouldn't want someone giving him a guitar, especially after he'd been caught stealing one. But, if Ruby gave her dad a guitar, surely he'd take it. At least he would if she'd earned it fair and square. What if they put on a concert—with Ruby— and charged people an entrance fee? Could they earn enough to buy a guitar? Maddie set her pencil down and climbed off the bed, so excited she forgot to be tired. She stopped halfway to the door. Plus, they could invite Annabeth and Emily to be in the concert—her friends would definitely want to help. And maybe if they worked together on the performance, whatever had been broken between them could be fixed. Emily had sent flowers last night, after all.

"I've got it, I've got it, I've got it!" she shouted, running downstairs.

"Whoa!" Mom caught her before she barreled into the kitchen island. "You've got what?"

"You always say music is like medicine," Maddie

began. "I think Ruby's dad needs a guitar, but it won't work for us to give him one."

"No, probably not," Mom said.

"But if we put on a concert and charge a quarter—or a dollar—we can raise money and buy him one. I mean, I know you and Dad could buy him a guitar, but I want to make my own difference. And I think it's important that Ruby has a chance to be part of this. For her and her dad's sake. So, we can invite her to be in our concert, and invite Annabeth and Emily too, and—"

"Maddie, that's a lot of ands," Mom said. "Honey, I don't want you to get your hopes up too high. We may not be able to make all that—"

"But don't you see, Mom?" Maddie interrupted. "I have to try. Ruby is my friend."

"What's going on?" Dad asked, coming up from the downstairs studio.

"Maddie wants to invite Ruby and some of the girls to put on a concert to raise money. She'd like to buy a guitar for Ruby's dad."

"It's not impossible, is it, Dad?" Maddie asked. "How much is a guitar, anyway?"

"We can probably find a solid used one for $200 or so," Dad said.

Maddie quickly did the calculations in her mind. "So, maybe we charge $5 for the concert. People would pay extra if they know the money is going to a good cause, right?"

She looked first at Mom and then at Dad. "Please?"

Dad was the first to start nodding. "I think it's a great idea, Mads. Rick is truly a fantastic guitarist, and I do think having his own guitar would make a difference for him. I was just downstairs thinking about how I might try to hook him up with a possible job, but . . ." He shook his head. "I think he has to do some work first. He has the skills to play, but his head and his heart have to be in the right place."

"Do you think he'd take the guitar, if it came from the kids—from Ruby?" Mom asked.

Dad winked at Maddie. "It's pretty difficult to turn down a gift from your daughter, that's for sure."

"So, we can call the shelter and invite Ruby over?" Maddie asked.

Mom took a deep breath. "And here I thought today was going to be a low-key, restful Saturday after the concert."

"So, yes?" Maddie pressed.

"Call in your sisters," Mom said. "They'll want to be in on the plan."

THIRTY-TWO

Everyone launched into motion. Mom got in touch with Ruby's mom and made arrangements to pick Ruby up and have her spend the night with the Glimmers. The concert would be tomorrow on the back lawn. Maddie went out to the backyard to explain her plan to Lulu and Mia. Lulu went to collect possible costumes, while Maddie and Mia walked up the street to do the hard part.

"Emily first," Maddie said. "She sent flowers last night."

"Agreed," Mia said.

Their friends both lived in the Glimmers' neighborhood. Emily's house was about halfway up the street, and Annabeth lived two houses past Emily. Most of the time, the girls were in and out of one another's houses, which had made this past week—and the space—all the more difficult.

Maddie knocked on Emily's door.

Emily's mom answered with her usual warm smile, an encouraging sign. "Hi there, girls. How was the concert last night?"

"We had a lot of fun," Mia said.

"But we missed Emily," Maddie added. "Is she home?"

"She's in the backyard with Annabeth. Would you girls like to go on through and see them?"

Maddie exchanged looks with Mia. It might have been easier to talk to their friends one at a time, but maybe it was better to get it over with all at once.

"Sure." Maddie let Mia lead the way, but caught her sister's arm before they went out onto the porch. "Let's not say anything about last night, unless they ask. Well—besides thanking Emily for the flowers."

"Right," Mia said, sliding open the glass door.

Emily and Annabeth sat side by side on swings. They glanced at one another when they saw the twins. For a second, Maddie wondered whether everything would go wrong again.

But then, Emily smiled. "Hey, we were just talking about you."

Maddie felt Mia tensing up beside her, but she decided to push ahead, ignoring her own worries, and the ones she knew Mia was having too. "Thank you for the sunflowers, Emily. They were beautiful."

"You liked them?" Emily's smile brightened, but then she looked at her feet. "I'm sorry I wasn't there last night. We called about tickets a couple hours before the show, but it was too late."

By now, Maddie and Mia had closed the distance between themselves and their friends. Annabeth stood up from her swing, took a deep breath, and blew it out.

Then she said, "I'm sorry too. What was it like, standing on the Opry circle? Was the show really sold out?"

Mia nodded, but held back from telling the girls every last detail. "We're actually here to see if you'd sing with us tomorrow."

"Sing? Tomorrow?" Emily asked.

"And maybe dance too," Maddie said. "We're putting on our own miniature benefit—in our backyard."

"What's it for?" Annabeth asked.

Maddie and Mia explained what had happened with the guitar, with Ruby's dad, and with Ruby herself.

"So what do you think?" Maddie asked.

"We could do our dance!" Emily said. "And we could all sing together—it would be so much fun, don't you think, Annabeth?"

"I'd love to help," Annabeth said. "And yes, it does sound fun."

"Before we go, though," Mia said. "I owe you both an apology. I was so excited to tell you about our summer and everything that I didn't stop to think about how you might feel. I didn't mean to leave you out, but I see how you could have felt that way."

"I'm sorry too," Maddie said. "I could see you were upset, and even though I wanted to, I couldn't figure out a way to make things better. At the very least, I should have said sorry right away."

Annabeth and Emily exchanged another of their looks, but this time they turned back to Maddie and Mia with matching smiles on their faces. Relief flooded through Maddie.

"When is Ruby coming over?" Annabeth asked.

"Any minute now," Mia answered.

"Should we go rehearse, then?" Annabeth asked.

Emily threw her arms around Maddie, and then around Mia, making things finally feel back to normal. Hugs from Emily, plans from Annabeth—everything the way it was supposed to be. They hurried home to introduce Annabeth and Emily to Ruby. With Ruby's help, the girls put together the most spectacular concert any of them could imagine. They worked up a couple instrumental songs. Mia played piano and Emily and Maddie played bongo drums. Ruby's dad had taught her how to play guitar, so she played some background chords. Lulu and Annabeth played harmonicas. Then, on other songs, Annabeth played the piano while everyone else sang. Annabeth and Emily's dance came midway through the show. Mia, Maddie, and Lulu added Ruby to their dance, which they used as the finale.

"Do you think people will actually pay $5 each for our concert?" Ruby wanted to know.

"I'm sure they will!" Annabeth showed the girls the flyer she'd made in between rehearsing the musical and dance numbers. "Let's copy these, and we can take them door to door."

By the time the sun was painting the clouds pink and orange, they'd invited everyone in the neighborhood, plus anyone else they could think of.

"I think we'll have at least 40 in the audience," Annabeth said.

"My dad is going to be so surprised," Ruby said. "I don't know how to thank you!"

"No need to thank us," Emily said. "This is fun!"

THIRTY-THREE

The sleepover with Ruby was hands down the most fun sleepover Maddie had ever had. The girls pitched a tent in the playroom and slept in sleeping bags so no one would be left out of the fun. Ruby played some of her favorite songs on the guitar—which were all Sunday school songs—and everyone sang along. They pretended a pile of red and orange pillows was a campfire, and Mom and Dad even let them make s'mores in the microwave to bring upstairs and eat as a late-night snack.

"But after your snack, lights out," Mom said. "You want to be rested for your concert tomorrow. What a musical weekend you girls have had!"

They snuggled into their sleeping bags and tried to go to sleep. But falling asleep wasn't easy, because whenever they started settling in, someone would whisper something. Then, they'd all start giggling and have to start quieting down all over again. Maddie's eyes felt dry as sandpaper when she finally let them close and drifted off to sleep.

When she woke up, she leapt out of her sleeping bag. The concert was at ten, and they had to set up chairs, put on costumes, eat breakfast, and get everything else set up. All the girls worked at a dead run until just before ten, when they found themselves standing near a tree in the backyard with Annabeth and Emily, watching the crowd gather.

They sang and danced their hearts out, and when the show was over, the crowd kept shouting for an encore. The girls decided to sing an impromptu version of "This Little Light of Mine" with Annabeth playing piano and Ruby on guitar. Then, the girls all took their final bows. The backyard audience gave them a whoop-filled standing ovation. Once the crowd had gone, the girls sat on the back porch and counted their earnings. $275—plenty to buy a guitar.

Mom and Dad took all the girls to the music store so they could pick out the guitar together. Ruby pointed out one that was black around the edges with red near the opening.

"What's that opening called, anyway?" Lulu wanted to know.

"It's called a sound hole," Dad said.

"That guitar looks just like the one my dad used to have," Ruby said.

"Then, that's the one we should buy." Dad lifted it down off the wall.

Ruby strummed a couple chords, and then nodded. "This one okay?" she asked the girls.

"Yes!" It was unanimous.

Ruby slid the pile of five-dollar bills across the counter. The guitar came with a case, and cost $223, so

they had enough to buy two extra sets of strings and a
tuner too.

Then they drove Ruby back to Third Street. As she
climbed out of the car, the guitar hugged to her chest,
she said, "You know where to find Dad most days. You'll
come and listen sometime, won't you?"

"Can we go tomorrow night?" Maddie asked.

"Let's plan to go on Saturday," Mom said. "That way
we give Rick a chance to settle in with his guitar. Plus,
you girls could use a few quiet evenings. It's been an
exciting week."

"I'll make sure to be there on Saturday then, too,"
Ruby said.

Maddie was relieved to not have to say good-bye
to Ruby forever. She gave her new friend a hug. "See
you soon!"

When Saturday finally came, the girls loaded up in
the car with Mom, Dad, and Miss Julia.

"What if he's not there?" Lulu asked.

"I called the shelter," Mom said. "Denise said that
Ruby and her family went out to the Opry today, so I'm
guessing he'll be there."

Sure enough, Ruby's dad had set up his guitar and
case on the steps, and was playing for a gathering crowd.

"He's so good!" Maddie said, as they crossed the
courtyard. "Don't you think, Dad?"

"Yes," Dad said. "I think helping him get the guitar
was the exact right thing to do, Maddie. Soon, I'm sure

he'll be ready to take on more, maybe even a job. I have a few ideas about how to help out with that when he's ready."

When Ruby spotted them, she ran over and gave everyone hugs. "He loves the guitar," she told them. "At first, I was worried. He wanted to know how I got it and whether I paid for it. Once I told him I'd earned the money with your help, he took the case into his arms and held it tight." Her eyes filled with tears, but she smiled through them. "And then, he started to play."

Maddie linked her arm through Ruby's. Ruby linked hers through Lulu's, and Lulu linked hers through Mia's. Then they all stood, listening, watching.

"I think he's back for good," Ruby whispered.

The happiness that had been growing inside Maddie ballooned, filling her from head to toe. This. This was the happy ending she'd been waiting for. She breathed deep, taking in the crisp fall air, the feel of her new friend by her side, and the bright notes of the guitar.

Ruby's dad kept right on playing.

London Art Chase

By Award-Winning Recording Artist Natalie Grant

In *London Art Chase*, the first title in the new Faithgirlz Glimmer Girls series, readers meet 10-year-old twins Mia and Maddie and their adorable little sister, Lulu. All the girls are smart, sassy, and unique in their own way, each with a special little something that adds to great family adventures.

There is pure excitement in the family as the group heads to London for the first time to watch mom, famous singer Gloria Glimmer, perform. But on a day trip to the National Gallery, Maddie witnesses what she believes to be an art theft and takes her sisters and their beloved and wacky nanny, Miss Julia, on a wild and crazy adventure as they follow the supposed thief to his lair. Will the Glimmer Girls save the day? And will Maddie find what makes her shine?

Available in stores and online!

A Dolphin Wish

*By Award-Winning Recording
Artist Natalie Grant*

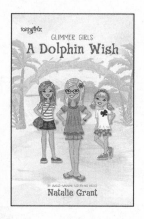

Join twins Mia and Maddie and their
sidekick little sister, Lulu, as they travel
the country finding adventure, mystery,
and sometimes mischief along the way.
Together with their famous mother,
singer Gloria Glimmer, and their slightly
wacky nanny Miss Julia, the sisters learn lessons about being
good friends, telling the truth, and a whole lot more.

In *A Dolphin Wish* — a three-night stop in the city of San Diego
seems like it might be just the break the girls need — lovely
weather and great sights to see. That is until they hear animal
handlers at Captain Swashbuckler's Adventure Park talking
about the trouble they've been having keeping the animals in
their habitats. Mia and her sisters cannot resist a challenge and
they talk Miss Julia into another visit to the educational amuse-
ment park to search for clues as to what or who is helping the
animals escape.

Available in stores and online!